The Cat at the Door

And Other Stories to Live By

Anne D. Mather
and
Louise B. Weldon

Illustrated by Lyn Martin

HAZELDEN®

First published June 1991.

ISBN: 0-89486-758-X

Printed in the United States of America.

Library of Congress Catalog Card Number: 91-70284

Editor's note:
   Hazelden Educational Materials offers a variety of information on chemical dependency and related areas. Our publications do not necessarily represent Hazelden programs, nor do they officially speak for any Twelve Step organization.

Contents

About the book:

The Cat at the Door and Other Stories to Live By illustrates the power of positive thinking in story form. The children in these stories suffer from stage fright and shyness, learn how to water-ski, dread the first day of school, move away from their friends, confide in their diary, and worry about what others think about them. They sometimes learn hard lessons but also learn about themselves. Most important, they learn to like themselves.

For parents who are trying to teach their children values but are not sure how to explain abstract concepts in terms their children can understand, *The Cat at the Door and Other Stories to Live By* at once offers the guidance of an inspirational book but the appeal of an illustrated storybook. Children will enjoy reading the stories on their own but will also benefit from discussing them with their parents. It is a book for the whole family to live by.

About the authors:

Anne Mather has been a professional writer for sixteen years. Her clients include the Center for Disease Control, the Task Force for Child Survival, and Emory University. She has written extensively on addiction issues and is the author of Bridging the Gap, a guide for teenagers.

Louise Weldon is a hypnotherapist whose clients include children and adolescents who are working to improve grades, behavior, and self-confidence. She also gives workshops on parenting skills and children's self-esteem.

Acknowledgments

We wish to thank our husbands and all of our friends and relatives for their enthusiastic support during the creation of this book. We cannot name you all, but we do wish to acknowledge Katherine Lord and Marie Cantlon for their honest evaluations and other invaluable help and direction; Guy Bishop, Charles Brooks, Sue Dean, Tom Dietsch, Candy Finley-Brooks, Debbie Holman, Mary Lamb, Dallas Snyder, Gail Torchio, Pat Waldoch, and Nancy Walker for being our "cheerleaders"; and Sam Ronnie and Dr. Kennedy Shultz for their constant inspiration and clear thinking. Finally, we wish to thank Hazelden—and in particular, our editors, Sid Farrar, Vince Hyman, Debora O'Donnell-Tavolier, and Jane Thomas—for their belief in and help with this book.

And Especially For

Jeannie, Maggie, and Rainbow
and All of Today's Children

I'm Smart at Being Me

Jimmy spent a lot of time comparing himself with his sisters and brothers or somebody at school. Sometimes he sized up his mother and father alongside his friend Matthew's parents. He was always trying to figure out who was "better" or "best."

One day Jimmy asked his mother, "Are cats smarter than dogs?"

"Cats are smart at being cats," Mom said. "Dogs are smart at being dogs. A cat couldn't be a dog, and a dog couldn't be a cat, so who cares who's smarter? They're both smart at being what they're supposed to be."

Jimmy and his mother ate cookies and talked about that idea. "You could never be a Matthew," she said, "all blond and neat. But nobody could ever be a Jimmy half as good as you. What do your friends especially like about you?"

Jimmy thought for a moment. "I'm nice to my friends. I don't boss them around."

We can admire other people for their special ways, enjoying their differences without trying to top them or wishing we were in their places. Life is not a contest. People are smart at being themselves.

Positive thought: I'm smart at being me. It's what I'm best at. It's what I was created for.

The Day the Cat Died

On Friday, Snugglepuss the cat disappeared. In the past, he had sometimes stayed outside all night, but he had always been waiting at the back door in the morning. When he didn't come back on Saturday, Dad and the children, Lou and Mary, went looking for him. They thought maybe he was stuck up a tree, but they couldn't find him.

Disappointed, they went home. Soon after, a neighbor called. "Have you been looking for your cat?" she asked. Then she told Dad she had found Snugglepuss dead by the road near her home.

At first, the children were shocked. They wailed. They sobbed. So did Mom. They had dearly loved Snugglepuss for almost five years.

All day Saturday they each were saying, "I can't believe it. I'll miss him so much." And tears would start again. The family canceled plans to go out to dinner. By evening, they were crying only sometimes, when the loss of Snugglepuss struck them freshly again like a wave on a seashore. The children went to bed early, and they snuggled their teddy bears closer than usual under their chins.

Positive thought: People need to feel their sadness before they can finish with it. Grief passes, but it takes time.

On Cats and Privacy

"One of the reasons I miss my cat so much," Mary said one day after Snugglepuss died, "is that I could tell him things I never tell anyone else."

"Is that so?" Mom said. She hadn't known that Mary talked to the cat.

"Yes, he was like a living diary," Mary said through her tears. "I told him everything. Now I can't do that."

Mom wondered out loud whether she was listening enough to Mary. "Am I talking too much and listening too little?" To Mom's surprise, Mary just shook her head. Mom understood now.

"You mean there are some thoughts you'd just like to keep to yourself?" she asked.

"Yes," said Mary. "And telling them to a pet is almost like talking them over with yourself."

Mary was talking about a need for privacy, a good, natural feeling.

Positive thought: I like to keep some of my thoughts to myself. I call this "liking my privacy." It's normal, and it's okay to feel this way.

Honest with God

One night Mary was so upset about the death of Snugglepuss that she even felt mad at God.

"Why did you need him with you?" she asked through her tears. "You're God. You're everywhere. So you get to see him all the time anyway. But now I can't play with him anymore."

The next day, Mary felt a little guilty about being mad at God. She talked to her parents about it.

"I don't think you have to worry about hurting God's feelings," Dad told Mary. "God understands how much you hurt right now. But you may need to forgive yourself for feeling so mad. Your anger is hurting you, not God."

Positive thought: I don't have to worry about being too honest with God. God can take it.

Deciding to Get a New Cat

No one wanted to get a new kitten right away after Snuggle-puss died. It just didn't seem right. It made the children feel disloyal, as if they were replacing him, which they knew they could never do. So they waited a while.

But then they started to yearn for a pet. Something to stroke at night . . . something to feel curled up at their feet . . . something to feed and be responsible for.

But there was one problem. Snugglepuss had been Mary's pet; she had chosen him for her birthday when she was a little girl. So if she got another cat, she wanted it to be *her* pet.

But Mary had a little brother now. Lou also wanted a pet to call his own.

"One pet for the whole family," Dad said.

"We'll all have to share," said Mom.

"But I'm the one who's lonesome for Snugglepuss," Mary cried. "I don't want to share a pet!" She went away to her bedroom and cried.

Mary remembered the way Snugglepuss used to rub against Mom's ankles and play with Lou's shoelaces and sleep on the back of Dad's chair while he read the newspaper. At bedtime, Snugglepuss curled up behind Mary's knees, but in the morning he was always asleep in his own basket. Cats could love everybody, she thought, but they didn't really belong to anybody.

5

At bedtime, when Dad kissed Mary and tucked her in, she said, "I can share the new kitten, Dad. But could I please name it?"

Dad smiled. "Sounds like a good idea to me," he said.

That night, for the first time since Snugglepuss died, Mary slept soundly.

Positive thought: Painful feelings slowly fade. I can work out ways to share the good things in life.

Little Brother's Birthday Gift

"Mom," said Lou while Mary was brushing her teeth after breakfast, "please let Mary have a kitten. Even if the new cat belongs to Mary, I can still play with him. Mary cries in the dark sometimes, thinking about Snugglepuss. Please, Mom."

Mom gave her seven-year-old a tighter hug than usual.

"I was thinking, Mom," Lou continued, "that I could give Mary the new kitten on her birthday. He could be my present."

"He certainly could," said Mom. "No one could give a better present than that, Lou, because you're giving your sister something you really wanted for yourself."

"The cat will be her favorite present," Lou said.

What made Mom so proud was that each of her children loved the idea of a cat so much that each was willing to give up "owning" it.

Positive thought: What goes around comes around. What I give to another person comes back to me, multiplied many times.

The Cat at the Door

The next morning, before the family could go to the pet store to get a new kitten, Mary opened the door to pick up the newspaper. A skinny gold and white cat dashed in out of the cold. He was meowing like crazy. Snugglepuss had never made that much noise, so everybody laughed.

They still had plenty of cat food, so Mary fed the stray. Lou turned to Dad and said, "It doesn't seem right to turn a stray away. Let's just keep him if we can't find the owner."

"Then you won't be able to give your sister a kitten for her birthday," said Dad.

"I don't care," said Lou. "I already love this one."

"I'd like to keep the stray too," said Mary.

"Then you won't be able to get a new little kitten," said Mom.

But Mary didn't mind. "We lost a cat, and now this cat has come to us," she said. "I think Snugglepuss sent him to us."

The family advertised in the paper: "Found. Skinny but beautiful gold and white cat." But the owner never called. Mary named the cat Faith to remind her to keep faith when she felt sad.

Positive thought: Sad times pass. Life is always giving us new opportunities to be happy again.

The Cat at the Door

The Big Pink Eraser

Jerry purchased a large pink eraser. It was as big as an entire pencil. On the top were written the words "For BIG Mistakes." He was glad to have such a big eraser because he made his share of mistakes in school.

Everyone makes mistakes in school and in other areas of life. Jerry can't just erase mistakes that he makes in life. But he does have choices about how to handle them.

He can criticize himself. He can go over and over the mistake in his mind. He can feel bad.

Or he can say to himself, "Okay. I made a mistake. I'm not going to do that again." He can forgive himself. He can make amends if he hurts someone else.

Positive thought: I handle mistakes in a way that is good for me. I let go of past mistakes and go on to something new.

Now Is Not Forever

John barely made it into the house and up to his room before he burst into tears. It was the most awful day of his life. The kids had picked teams for baseball during recess, and he was chosen last. Then when he actually hit the ball—a miracle—he ruined it all by stealing a base and getting caught.

"Why'd you do that, man?" a teammate asked him. "You ruined it for us."

"I blew my chance to be a good baseball player," John wailed. "Now I'll never get to play baseball, and all those guys are going to think I'm a jerk."

John didn't know that bad things don't last forever. Even if the guys think John is a jerk today, they may not tomorrow, and by next week, nobody will even remember the mistake—except John, if he keeps reliving it in his mind.

Even though something hurts a lot now, the pain will pass. Parents or older brothers and sisters can tell children memories of awful troubles that went away as they grew up—things like zits, or fights with a brother or sister, or lots of homework. Troubles come to everybody, but troubles don't last.

Positive thought: Bad things don't last. And I can handle them until they go away.

The Worry Dolls

Guatemala, a country in Central America, has a tradition that helps children give up worrying. Each child receives a small handwoven bag with six tiny handmade dolls inside. Each is no bigger than the child's thumb.

At night when a child feels worried, he takes out a worry doll and tells her about it. If more than one problem troubles him, he gives another doll his second worry. The dolls stay out of their little purse for the night, holding the child's worries for him so he can sleep.

Children can make their own "worry dolls" by painting clothes on Popsicle sticks or dressing twigs with scraps of colored cloth. They really do work—not because the dolls hold the worries, but because God does.

Positive thought: I trust in a Higher Power, God, and let go of my fears. Free of fear, I feel peaceful and can rest.

Teddy Bears at the Party

Kris had packed her bag for the slumber party, but before carrying it downstairs, she gave her big teddy bear, Puffy, one more squeeze.

"I can't take you with me," she said. "I'm going to be with other girls my age, and they might think it's babyish to have a teddy bear."

She had a lot of fun at the party: pizza, dress-up, a video. But around midnight, when Kris and a few other girls were ready to hit the sack, Kris saw her girlfriend Susan take a bedraggled teddy bear out of her suitcase.

Susan saw Kris staring and said, "I know I'm supposed to be too grown-up for him, but I'm not. And I don't ever want to be."

Kris knew exactly what she meant. And next time, she decided, she would bring Puffy along.

Positive thought: I am proud of the things and people that make me happy, that I love. I don't apologize for them.

I Can Talk to God About Anything

Some people worry that they might be praying for something too small to bother God with. They feel they should pray only for big things—like a cure for cancer or an end to war.

It *is* good to pray for such things, but God doesn't look for the most "worthy" cause before answering prayers. You don't have to be swamped with troubles to get God's attention.

God, our Higher Power, loves all creatures, "great and small," and will handle problems of any size.

Positive thought: No matter how small my problem is, it's big enough to upset me. So I talk to God about it.

The Special Plate

A unt Beth and the family sent the Johnsons a "special plate" for a family present. It was brightly colored, like fireworks on the Fourth of July. "Use this dinner plate to honor somebody on birthdays and other special occasions," said the card.

The Johnsons used the plate the first time when Amy made the gymnastics team. She beamed when she saw the pretty plate in front of her chair. All through the meal, she felt that her family had chosen her to be the star.

The next special occasion was Sara's birthday. Once again, the plate worked such magic that the Johnsons began to use it more often. One day, for example, when Dad had worked hard all day in the yard, Mom and the kids put the plate at his place.

"Oh, so I'm the special one tonight, huh?" he said, winking at the girls. He seemed to enjoy this attention and the fact that they had all noticed the work he had done.

The next time, Dad put the plate at Mom's place when she finished a sweater she had been knitting for a long time.

"You know, I think we're going to wear out this special plate," Mom said, laughing. "Maybe we need more than one. I guess we're all pretty special." And it was true.

Positive thought: I'm special. So is every member of my family.

Rich Breakfasts

Jeannie and Darin usually ate cold cereal every morning. In fact, every payday Dad stocked the pantry with several different kinds. For a week the kids could choose among their old favorites, plus something new that Dad had found on the shelf at the grocery store. When the other cereal boxes were empty, they all ate corn flakes again.

One morning, however, Mom made scrambled eggs. She served them in a warm buttered roll with homemade applesauce on the side.

While both children were gobbling up this treat, Jeannie said, "I feel like I'm rich when we have hot stuff for breakfast."

Mom and Dad burst out laughing. Dad said, "That sounded funny, Jeannie, because some people think you need a lot more to be rich. Today, people think 'rich' means having a lot of money. It doesn't necessarily mean that. Being rich starts with feeling happy and thankful for what you've got. And you *do* have a lot. I'm glad you know it."

Positive thought: I'm very thankful for all the riches I have in my life. I *am* rich.

The New Stepmom

Carolyn's dad divorced her mom last year. Recently, he married someone else. Carolyn likes her dad's new wife, Margaret, and enjoys visiting them on weekends. Sometimes she feels disloyal for liking Margaret so much. She *really* doesn't want her mom to know she likes Margaret.

Relationships with new stepparents can bring up a lot of different feelings. Being the kid in the middle sometimes feels awkward. But liking and enjoying a stepparent does *not* mean that a child loves her other parent any less.

It's okay for Carolyn to love and enjoy her new stepmom. And as time goes on, she'll be more comfortable with her feelings.

Positive thought: I always have room in my life to love another person.

Best Friends

"Amanda is so much fun. Do you know what she did today?" That was Shannon talking, and Mom just had to laugh at her question. For as long as Shannon and Amanda had been friends, Shannon had been giving her family reports on all the funny things that Amanda did.

The family had all heard stories about the high, silly laugh that Amanda faked to get everyone laughing. Or about the way she said, "I just crack myself up," when she told a joke. Or how she could imitate a snobby British lady, saying "Tah tah, my deah."

And now Shannon was off again—her eyes twinkling, her voice breaking as she told another Amanda story. Nobody was as bold and funny as Amanda. Their friendship made Shannon feel that someone outside her own family understood her and loved her just the way she was.

Positive thought: It's fun to have a best friend.

God, Are You Mad at Me?

Mandy loved the friendship and challenge of gymnastics, but this year the coach cut her from the beginners' team. The loss hurt. She cried and cried.

Even worse, most of her friends *did* make the team again. At lunch now, all the gymnasts hung around together. It seemed as if they didn't like her as much anymore.

One night Mandy said, "Mom, I wonder whether God is mad at me. That would explain why all these bad things are happening."

Mom sighed. "Mandy, I want to be honest with you. You've had some hard punches lately. I don't want to act like they can just be brushed away like tears.

"But honey, I think *you're* the one that's mad, not God. And when you say your friends don't like you anymore, I think it's more that *you're* disappointed with *them* right now. You don't feel like they're being sensitive to you."

Mandy started crying. "I am mad," she yelled. "At the coach and at my friends."

"I don't blame you," Mom said, tears in her eyes. "Let's do something to get the angry feelings out—have a pillow fight or something. I know you'll bounce back from this setback once you've gotten over the anger and the hurt."

Positive thought: I have a right to be angry sometimes.

18

Heroes

Everybody has a hero, a model to learn from and believe in. That kind of admiration is one of the sweetest blessings in life.

Young children often choose imaginary people as heroes—someone like Wonderwoman. As young people grow up, their heroes are usually real people—a favorite teacher, a coach, or a famous person like Mother Teresa.

Even grown-ups have heroes. All of us want to know more than we know, do more than we do, be greater than we are. Heroes are proof that human beings can achieve such dreams. Heroes are our hope.

To *be* someone's hero is, of course, a great compliment. But *having* a hero is our compliment to ourselves. It shows that we have grown up enough to know that we don't know everything and that we want to do and be more than we are right now. This honesty is a sign of maturity.

Positive thought: My heroes are proof that I can be what I want to be.

Being a Friend to Myself

Terry Stuckey's mother couldn't believe what she heard coming from Terry's room.

"You're so stupid!" she heard her son say. "That's the dumbest thing you've ever done. All you do is mess things up!"

His mom wondered which friend Terry was treating so rudely. She hadn't heard Robbie, the boy next door, come in, but who else could it be?

A little while later Mom asked Terry why he was saying such cruel things to his friend.

Terry was a little surprised that she had heard him. "Oh, I wasn't talking to Robbie," Terry said. "I was talking to myself. I wouldn't talk to a friend what way. That would be an awful way to . . ." Terry stopped mid-sentence as he realized he would *never* talk to a friend the way he had talked to himself.

Terry forgot for a moment who his best friend really is.

Positive thought: I treat myself every bit as nicely as I treat a friend.

Learning to Say No

"Phil always asks to borrow my bike," Ben told his dad one day while they were cleaning out the garage. "It drives me crazy. Phil has his own bike; he just likes my ten-speed better. How can I say no to Phil without making him mad?"

"Saying no nicely is so hard for most people that adults actually take courses in it!" said Dad as he hung up the broom and brushed his hands together. "Try saying three things to Phil. First, tell him that you know what he wants. Second, tell him how you feel about that. Finally, ask him not to do the things that bother you anymore. Even when this answer doesn't work for me, I don't have to spend a lot of time thinking of things I wish I had said."

Next day at the park, Ben got a chance to try out Dad's advice.

"Look," said Ben. "I know you really like riding my bike. But I get upset when other people ride it. So please don't ask me to borrow it anymore."

"Well, if that's the way you feel about it, fine!" said Phil impatiently, and he sped away around a bend in the path.

But when Ben rode around the curve, Phil was waiting for him. "I'll race you to the pond," said Phil with a smile.

Positive thought: I have a right to say no. I can learn to say no comfortably.

A Difficult Friend

Natalie had a friend, Greg, who could be very difficult. Sometimes Greg got angry and tried to boss the other kids around. Sometimes he acted so sure of himself that Natalie wanted to scream.

"I know this is hard to believe," Mom said. "But people who act that sure of themselves usually feel the opposite way. They're just covering up. They're scared to let you know that they don't know everything."

Natalie thought for a minute. "It's pretty hard to feel sorry for someone who's being mean to you," she said.

"You can say that again," said Mom, laughing. "So why feel sorry for him? That's like worrying. When Greg gets angry and bossy, try doing a couple of things to deal with it.

"You can think of one thing you really like about Greg—just one. Remember that he can also be fun or helpful or whatever makes you feel a little better." Mom gave Natalie a hug. "Or you can just refuse to think about him for a while. Later, when he's feeling better about *himself,* he'll probably act nicer to *you.*"

Positive thought: Going over and over a mean thing someone did to me just upsets me. I can choose to think about something else.

Handling a Teaser

Kevin sat on Mark's baseball hat after the game and wouldn't give it back. After dropping Kevin off at his house, Dad said, "I noticed Kevin was teasing you all through the game."

"Yeah, he does that all the time," said Mark. "I know he's only joking, but it bugs me just the same, and I don't know what to do about it."

"He probably learned teasing at home," said Dad. "He's imitating somebody else—his parents, maybe, or an older brother or sister. He probably doesn't know how much it bothers you. A friend wouldn't deliberately do something to hurt you.

"Next time Kevin picks on you," Dad went on, "be honest with him. Say something like, 'I know you're teasing, but I don't want you to say those things to me. Please don't do that anymore'"

Mark practiced saying that to his dad until he felt comfortable with the words.

"It's okay to express how you feel and what you would like to happen in a situation," Dad said. "Being open and honest will help your friendship grow."

Positive thought: It's okay to say how I feel. Honesty builds good friendships.

23

Dancing Butterflies

"There go those butterflies again," Rachel said to her mother as they drove to ballet class.

"What butterflies? I don't see any," her mother said.

"The butterflies in my stomach!" Rachel exclaimed. "When it's close to recital time, I get butterflies on the way to class. They feel like they're just flapping their wings off."

Rachel became very quiet for a few minutes. Her mother wondered what was going on in her mind.

"It's okay now, Mom," she said. "I just put pretty little pink ballet slippers on the butterflies and watched them dance a quiet ballet. Now I'm calm."

Positive thought: When I'm nervous, I find ways to calm myself down.

Dancing Butterflies

The New Pen

M olly gave her new pen to Kelly even though she had wanted to keep it. She wasn't even sure why, except that Kelly's constant hinting had made her uncomfortable.

"Maybe I should give her the pen," Molly remembered thinking. "It would please Kelly. And it would be a nice thing to do." So she gave away her new pen.

And she felt awful afterwards. She couldn't get that pretty black and turquoise pen out of her mind. Why didn't she feel good?

She talked to her older sister Cathy about it. "I think it's good to do nice things for other people," Cathy said. "But you should feel good inside about giving. If you don't, listen to that bad feeling—it's telling you something.

"The next time something like this happens," Cathy continued, "ask yourself, 'Do I feel good about this? Am I doing this because I want to?' If you can't answer yes, don't do it."

"So now I gave away my pen, and I'm stupid besides," said Molly.

"No," said Cathy. "You're smarter now. You've learned that giving *in* isn't the same as giving. And you've learned to trust yourself—that part of you that felt uncomfortable when you were being pressured. Learning *that* is worth a lot more than a pen."

Positive thought: I'm learning, day by day, to trust myself and my feelings.

Dr. Kid

James had a bad cold, so his mom took him to the health clinic. When Dr. Rodriguez came in the room, James asked, "Are you going to make me well?"

Dr. Rodriguez looked at James for a minute. Then he said, "You may be surprised to hear this, James, but *you* are the one who makes yourself well."

"You mean that I'm a doctor too?" James asked.

"Absolutely," said Dr. Rodriguez. "Everybody is."

Dr. Rodriguez explained that James's fever was his body's way of reacting to his cold. Right now, whole armies of white blood cells were fighting his illness. Each day, without his even being aware of it, James's body fought off germs. Only once in a while did this army inside him fail. Then James got sick.

"I'm here to help you at those times," Dr. Rodriguez said. "But even now, I'm just helping your body heal itself. When your mom puts a Band-Aid on a cut, the Band-Aid doesn't cure you, does it? It just helps the body help itself. That's what I do. And it's what you can help do too, Dr. Kid."

Positive thought: I can help my body heal itself.

In Charge of Me

Nine-year-old Gabriel had asthma. That was the fancy name the nurse at the clinic gave it. Before she told him what it was called, he thought everybody had trouble breathing sometimes.

Besides giving his trouble a name, the asthma clinic taught Gabe what things caused his wheezing. Causes differ from person to person—some people react to a pet cat or dog, some to bubble bath, others to tree pollen in the spring. Gabe started keeping a diary to notice what his "triggers" were.

Then the nurse taught him how to "read" his body. Gabe thought that idea was pretty funny. "I've only read books before," he told the nurse.

But soon he understood that when he read his body, he noticed what was happening to it. A sore throat or an itchy feeling could be clues that he was going to have trouble breathing soon. Knowing that, he could get help early. Then he wouldn't panic.

By learning about asthma and how it worked in his body, Gabe helped control it. He didn't get sick as often. And when he did, he didn't feel so scared. Gabe liked learning about and being in control of himself and his illness.

Positive thought: I like to learn about things that affect me. Knowledge helps me to control my life.

A Girl Named Selamawit

You may find it hard to pronounce her name, but Selamawit is famous.

When she was four years old, someone found her in the streets of Addis Ababa, a big Ethiopian city. They asked her what she wanted to be when she grew up.

"I want to be alive," she said.

They took a picture of her and made it into a poster. The question they had asked her and her stunning answer were also on the poster. It became famous the world over. Thinking of Selamawit, people banded together to tell the world that children should have the right to survive to adulthood.

Since this child survival movement started in the 1980s, battles in El Salvador and Lebanon have been stopped to let children be given vaccines that will prevent them from dying of certain diseases. Even presidents of countries have joined in the effort to destroy childhood diseases like polio and measles.

And today, Selamawit is still alive. As of this writing, she is ten years old, second in her third-grade class of one hundred children.

Five words from a child helped start a revolution: a revolution for healthy children the world over. That's how powerful words are.

Positive thought: My words are powerful.

The Chain of Love

Yaquita and her second-grade classmates are making a chain of love to go around their classroom. The children have several strips of construction paper that are 1 1/2 inches long. They are writing wonderful ideas about themselves on each strip.

Cory writes "I am lovable" on a blue strip of paper.

Rita decorates her paper with a smiley face. Then she writes, "I feel good about me."

Candy and Donna are best friends, so they make a link saying "Best Friends" and write their names on it.

Yaquita puts a drop of glue on her strip of paper and carefully glues the ends together to form a circle. The other children add their strips, and a colorful chain is formed. Each week they will decorate new strips to add to the chain until it is long enough to go around the entire room.

Positive thought: I surround myself with loving ideas about myself.

When "Three's a Crowd"

Whenever Stephanie or her big sister had a friend over, Stephanie ended up in tears. "Nobody likes me," she told her mother.

"Did you ever hear the expression 'Three's a crowd?'" Mom asked. "It means that when three people are playing, one may feel left out."

Stephanie saw that her mother understood. They figured out some different thoughts that might help when Stephanie felt ignored.

"I could say, 'I like myself' or 'My friends like me,'" Stephanie said.

"How about, 'My sister and I can share friends?'" Mom chimed in. "Or, 'A friend can disagree with me and still like me.'"

Stephanie repeated these statements several times until they sounded familiar. Saying them seemed to make her feel better. Because she didn't want to forget these thoughts, she also had the idea to write them down in a little spiral notebook. She put them on a separate page under the heading "Part I: Stephanie's Thoughts."

"When I get worried about sharing friends, I'm going to read these," Stephanie said. And she did.

Positive thought: Reminding myself of good things about myself makes me feel better about myself and others.

30

Gearing Up for Headgear

Noreen had to get braces. She had "braced herself" for this. She had even convinced herself that braces were cool. Lots of kids in her class had them. So when she went to the orthodontist's office, she was even a little excited.

Then Dr. Samson said, "Noreen, I'd like you to wear a headgear." Noreen's heart stopped.

"What does it look like?" she asked. Dr. Samson showed her. It was a piece of wire that went from her teeth around her head. In the back was a pad that stretched across her neck.

"This isn't much fun for an eleven-year-old to wear," Dr. Samson said, "because it's kind of weird-looking. But it will really help you a lot. I want you to wear it because I like you. And because you're pretty and this will help you stay that way."

Noreen gulped. "How long do I have to wear it?" she asked.

"That depends upon you," Dr. Samson said. "Usually more than a year—if you wear it only at night. But one girl wore it day and night, and was totally out of it in nine months."

Noreen smiled. It made her feel better to know what to expect and also to know that someone else had made a game out of wearing it. She would be okay with this new challenge.

Positive thought: How something affects me depends upon how I accept it.

First Day of Headgear

Well, "HG Day" had finally struck. Headgear Day. The orthodontist had given Noreen the new appliance.

"You could wear it only at night and after school for a while until you're used to it," the orthodontist had said. But Noreen decided to wear it to school right away. And some surprising things happened.

A sweet girl in the hall stopped Noreen and said, "Don't worry. My sister Lana has one of those too."

The class cutup made a joke about the headgear being a muzzle to stop Noreen from talking so much. Noreen and everybody else laughed.

Another friend said, "I have to go into one of those next month." Being an example for her friends *really* made Noreen feel good, because she was the only one in the fifth grade wearing a headgear.

Another friend asked, "Does it hurt?" (It did a little.)

Dad used the occasion to make all sorts of horrible puns, like "bracing up for braces" and "Are you geared up for this?"

At the end of HG Day, Noreen realized she had actually enjoyed the jokes as much as the kindness.

Positive thought: I'm proud of myself when I meet a new challenge. And I notice and appreciate how many people support me at such times.

Word Watch

The back door banged behind Joel. With a sigh of relief, he put his loaded backpack on the kitchen counter. He was thinking of what snack he could squeeze in before soccer practice when his dad yelled down, "Joel, hurry up. We need to go get new shoes before practice."

"Oh no," Joel groaned. He was starting to feel jumpy and exhausted at the same time, the way he felt when he'd eaten too many brownies. He looked at the homework crammed in his bag. "How am I going to get everything done tonight?" he wondered.

Joel's older brother Dave took one look at Joel's face and grinned. "You look like you're overwhelmed," he said.

"What does that mean?" Joel asked.

"It's the feeling you get when too much is happening, and too much is asked of you. You've got to do a hundred things, but you don't feel like doing one." Dave said.

"Boy, does that hit the nail on the head," Joel said. He was relieved that there was a word for what he was feeling. That meant that other people sometimes felt "overwhelmed" too. For some reason, this made him feel better. He wasn't nuts, for one thing. Or alone.

Positive thought: Words are important. Describing my feelings helps me accept them—and myself.

What Knitting and Thomas Edison Have in Common

Sue and Bets, seven and ten years old, love to knit. Although most craft books say that there are only two stitches—knitting and purling—Sue and Bets know better. There's a third: ripping up. Unraveling. Every knitter has to rip up mistakes and start again. In the end, it's worth it.

Sue and Bets have learned a secret that has helped many great people succeed. For example, Thomas Edison, the man who invented the light bulb, the moving picture, and the record player, knew a lot about starting over. But he didn't see it as failure.

"We're making real progress," he told friends after one thousand failures to make a light bulb. "We know a thousand ways it can't be done. We're that much closer to getting there."

Sue and Bets have something in common with the great inventor: sometimes backing up is part of moving forward.

Positive thought: Unsuccessful attempts can be looked upon as failures—or as lessons. Instead of thinking, "I failed," I'm going to think, "I learned a lot today."

I Don't Put Myself Down

"I can't believe what my mouth has done to my body," Alex said jokingly one day. This was his way of saying he had put on a few extra pounds around his middle.

His funny remark is a pretty good description not only of how people get fat, but also of how we get nervous or sad or mad.

Alex's mouth—or more accurately, his words, and of course, the thoughts behind those words—control his emotions and life as surely as what he eats determines the size of his body.

When he talks unkindly to himself *about* himself, reviewing all his mistakes and scolding himself for them, he's building self-hatred and shame.

And the way Alex talks about himself to others is just as bad. He thinks the only way to give someone else a compliment is to put himself down. He often says things like what he said when Janice won the school track meet: "You're the best runner in the school," he said. "I'll *never* be any good at running."

Alex's main job is to be his own best friend, not to tear himself down with unkind words.

Positive thought: My words can be my best friends or my worst enemies. They create my life, my feelings, and my experience.

Trusting Life

"Daddy, is it hard being a grown-up?" Taylor asked one day. Dad had to think a moment, because there *are* times in everybody's life when things are not as easy as we would like.

"No, for me, being a kid was harder," said Dad thoughtfully. "To me, the hardest part about life was being afraid. Afraid that I couldn't handle something. Or afraid that something bad in my life was going to last forever. Or afraid that I'd never have a close friend or something like that. But now I don't have those fears anymore."

"Why not?" asked Taylor. He was afraid he'd never learn to ride a bike, or be able to stand up to a bully at school.

"Well, life is full of lessons. Something is hard until you figure it out; then that part isn't hard anymore. After you've lived awhile and had more and more lessons, you finally understand that you *will* be able to handle things . . . that bad things *don't* last forever . . . that you *will* always have someone who loves you.

"What I'm saying, Taylor," Dad went on, "is that pretty soon you will start to see that life works out. Life is basically good. When you really believe that, your fears start to disappear. And without fear, life is not really hard—challenging, maybe, but no longer scary."

Positive thought: I don't have to be afraid of life. Life is good.

Laughitis

Rainbow and her mother were having their nighttime chat, as they always did before bed.

Sharing stories with her mom about her school day, Rainbow said, "Mom, Debbie is contagious."

"Oh, what does she have?" Mom asked.

Rainbow laughed and said, "Debbie has laughitis."

Rainbow went on to say that she had gone to class angry that day because some girl had pushed her on the playground. But Debbie had cheered her up by making her laugh. Then they had *both* gotten the giggles. Rainbow said she had ended up happy all day because she had "caught" Debbie's laughter.

Instead of catching a disease, she had caught a laugh!

Positive thought: Happiness is contagious. I am happy.

Making Lunches

Seven-year-old Steven was making his lunch for school: a peanut butter and jelly sandwich, juice, cookies, and an orange. While he was making his sandwich, he remembered something that had happened at school.

"Mom," he said, "when I told the kids at school that I make my own lunch, do you know what they said?"

"No," Mom answered.

"They said you must be *mean,*" Steven said.

Mom looked up. This was getting interesting. "What'd you say to that?" Mom asked.

"I told them that it's fun to make my lunch and that everybody should help out at home."

Right on, Steven!

Positive thought: I like doing some things for myself. I'm a part of my home, and I do my share.

Hugging Away Nightmares

M r. and Mrs. Brown woke up at four o'clock in the morning and found eight-year-old Jeremy standing in the dark at the foot of the bed.

"I had a nightmare," he said, his voice trembling.

"Come crawl into bed with us," said Dad. Jeremy snuggled up against his dad and soon fell asleep, calm now.

Jeremy's dad and mom understood that fear is a very powerful force. Some people think it causes most of the bad things people do. It's fear of not having enough money that causes some people to steal. It's fear their friends won't like them that causes many teenagers to smoke or drink. It's fear of punishment that causes children to lie about something they accidentally broke.

But love is stronger than fear. Dad's loving hug in the night canceled out Jeremy's nightmare. Love can erase hurt, ease pain.

Love is the greatest power in the universe. And everybody has that power!

Positive thought: A hug in the night can erase a nightmare. Love is always stronger than the things I fear.

Practical Jokes

In school one morning, Jim finished writing a love note to Sherry—signing it not from himself, but from Ned. Then he carefully folded it and asked Ned to hand it to Sherry.

"This is going to be really funny," he thought. Well, it was funny—to everyone but Sherry and Ned. To them, it was an awful joke.

Laughing and having fun is one of the good things in life. But laughing at someone else's expense can turn humor into hurt.

Jim could have used the Golden Rule when he considered a practical joke. That rule would have told him to treat others as he would like to be treated. He could've asked himself how he would feel if Ned signed such a note with Jim's name. If Jim would feel bad, then he shouldn't play the trick on Ned. It's that simple.

Positive thought: Today I treat others as I would like to be treated.

One Way to Forgive

Dad was out of town, so Erica was sleeping with Mom. Or trying to. She'd been tossing and turning since she'd gone to bed.

"Erica, you still haven't gotten over being mad at Jessica, have you?" Mom asked.

"No. I'm sick and tired of her, Mom," Erica said. "Friends are *not* supposed to hang up the phone on each other. It's rude."

"I agree," said Mom. "But you handled it well. You were angry and you told her so. Now I think you need to forgive and forget."

"I hate that word *forgive,*" Erica said.

"How about saying 'let go' instead?" Mom said. "That's what forgive means."

"I don't know how to do that," Erica said.

"Try this," Mom said. "Get real quiet and make a picture in your mind of Jessica. Imagine just one good thing happening to her—something you know she'd really like."

"Jessica would like to be more popular, Mom," said Erica. "So I see her surrounded with friends. Her phone is ringing off the hook, and she's grinning from ear to ear."

"And how are *you* feeling right now, Erica?" Mom asked.

"Better," said Erica.

"Then let's get some sleep," Mom said, turning off the light.

Positive thought: I can learn to forgive people.

I Forgive

"Does a person have to say 'I'm sorry' for us to forgive her?" Jay asked his father one night.

"Well, I know it's a lot nicer when you get an apology," his dad said. "But it really isn't necessary. Forgiveness is something we do for ourselves."

"What do you mean?" Jay asked.

"When you forgive, you let go of your own bad feelings about someone," Dad explained. "The other person is not required to do anything. She may not even know you have forgiven her."

Positive thought: Today I forgive someone I am angry with. I'll feel better because I did this.

Forgiving Begins at Home

Last night, Erin really embarrassed herself by arguing too loudly with her friend at the pizza parlor. She had really "lost her cool," and now she was embarrassed just thinking about it.

This morning Erin admitted her fault to herself. Because she was feeling so ashamed, she decided to talk herself out of that feeling.

"I can think of some really silly and even obnoxious things that I've seen friends do," Erin said to herself. "I don't dwell on their mistakes. And I don't point out their mistakes to them or ride them about it. In fact, I pretty much forget about them. So I'm going to do that for myself today."

Erin decided it wasn't the end of the world if she hadn't seemed as cool as she'd like to be.

"I'm going to forgive myself and quit thinking about this," she said. And she did.

Positive thought: I forgive myself for social embarrassments and even more serious mistakes. I quit thinking about them. Now.

The Blade of Grass

One spring day, Chad was cleaning up the den. To his surprise, he discovered a small blade of grass growing in between the baseboard and the carpet in the house!

"That's a strange place for grass to grow," he thought to himself. "It must have taken a lot of strength for it to grow up through the foundation and into our house. What a powerhouse!"

"I'm going to remember that blade of grass the next time I have a difficult project to complete or when I'm having trouble reaching a goal. I *know* I have as much strength and power within me as that tiny blade of grass has inside it," Chad thought.

Positive thought: I have the strength and power to accomplish whatever I want to do.

The New Cousin

Kurt stays with his Aunt Shirley after school each day. She's his favorite aunt. She seems like his second mother. But he's afraid that might change soon. Aunt Shirley is going to have a baby.

One afternoon when they were having an after-school snack, Kurt said to his aunt, "I don't know if I'm going to like having a baby around. I won't get all of your attention anymore."

Aunt Shirley could tell that Kurt had been thinking a lot about the new baby. She was glad he had shared what he was thinking. Kurt was her only nephew and the only grandchild in the family. Everybody loved him and gave him lots of attention.

"That's a real worry, Kurt," Aunt Shirley said. "When new babies are born, they get lots and lots of attention. Everybody oohs and aahs over them. It seems they can do no wrong. Sometimes other kids feel left out.

"But I love you, Kurt," she went on to say. "I know my baby will take up a lot of time, but I'll make time for my favorite nephew too.

"Here's how you can help," she continued. "Whenever you feel left out, tell me. You'll always be special to me. And you know what? You'll be special to this new baby too. The baby will be someone new to share love with." She gave Kurt a hug and a smile.

Positive thought: I feel good because I am loved. I share my love.

No Comparison

Jason is a straight-A student in middle school. He is also on the school track and baseball teams.

His younger brother, Keith, is an average student who has no interest in sports. It used to bother Keith when people told him that his brother was "a hard act to follow." Then one day he made up his mind that he didn't have to follow Jason at all.

Keith developed interests of his own. He enjoys reading about wild animals and painting them in their natural environment.

It doesn't bother him anymore when someone compares him with Jason. In fact, he made up a little rhyme that he repeats to himself when this happens:

> I'm good at this,
> Jason's good at that.
> We both have things
> We're very good at.

As Keith learned to accept himself for what he is instead of being sorry for what he isn't, others also began to notice his special talents. They think of him as Keith now, not just Jason's brother.

Positive thought: I don't have to follow in anyone else's footsteps. I am my own leader.

Gramps and the Mind Garden

Tim enjoyed spending spring holidays with his grandparents in the country. He always helped them plant their family garden. In the mornings, they got up early and prepared the soil. Then they planted the seeds. Tim loved seeing the results of his effort. Seeds would usually begin to sprout before he went back to his city apartment.

While they were working in the garden, Gramps would teach Tim things to help *him* grow too.

One day Gramps held up several watermelon seeds and said, "Tim, the thoughts in your mind grow and bear fruit just like these watermelon seeds. Your mind is like a garden, and your thoughts are the seeds. A good time to plant these seeds in your mind is at night before you go to bed. The crops that grow as a result of planting 'thought seeds' are the good things that happen in your life.

"I know how you like to see results," Gramps told Tim, "so why don't you plant some good thought seeds each night before you go to sleep and see what good things grow in your life from those thoughts?"

Positive thought: Each night before I go to sleep, I plant good thoughts in the garden of my mind.

Scarecrow

When Maryann saw the crows eating the corn seeds she and her brother Dick had planted in the family's vegetable garden, the children asked Dad to help them build a scarecrow.

"That's a good idea," said Dad. He drove a narrow board into the ground in the center of the garden, with a crossbar for shoulders and arms. Dick put the scarecrow's arms through the sleeves of Dad's worn-out plaid shirt. Maryann put an old hat at the top and hung a bell from the scarecrow's hand.

Then the children hid behind the shed to watch. They saw that the crows stayed away. The corn grew tall that summer, and they enjoyed eating it at harvesttime.

Minds are gardens too, always growing new ideas. Everything people have ever made or done began with an idea in somebody's mind.

But ideas need protection and time to grow, just as corn does. Negative thoughts such as "You can't do that" or "That won't work" are like crows that eat away at good ideas. Sometimes a child can be his own scarecrow by shooing away these pesky thoughts. Then his good idea can grow safely.

Positive thought: I take care of my ideas and let them grow.

Mom Tells the Truth

C hristy and Susan were comparing their moms. "I really like it when my mom tells me the truth about what she thinks," Christy said. "When I ask her how she likes my hair, she lets me know if she doesn't like it."

"Doesn't that hurt your feelings?" Susan wondered. "It would hurt mine if I'd spent a long time fixing my hair."

"Not at all," Christy answered. "She's just giving her opinion. Once she didn't care for the style. Well, I wore it that way for a few days anyhow because it looked so grown-up. *I* liked the style, you know?"

Christy was glad her mom respected her enough to tell her the truth. "I wouldn't like it if she faked it because she was afraid of hurting my feelings," Christy said.

Positive thought: I like it when people are honest with me.

Unanswered Prayers

Jenny came to her mom crying. "I said a prayer today, and it didn't work," she sobbed.

"What was your prayer?" Mom asked.

"I prayed that Stephanie would ask me to her party. And she didn't."

"That must be scary," said Mom. "Does it seem that God isn't listening or doesn't care?"

Jenny nodded.

"Maybe there's another explanation. When we pray to make somebody else do something we want, a lot of times the answer we get is no," said Mom.

"When you have a problem, try asking what *you* can do to make a situation better. Your answer may come as a thought. Or it may come in something a friend says to you."

Positive thought: My prayers are answered. But sometimes I have to be willing to change a little to hear the answer.

Helping a Friend

Patrick's good friend Jed had been feeling really low. He was sad because his parents weren't getting along very well.

It seemed that nothing Patrick did could help Jed. Patrick tried to cheer up his friend, but it did no good. He felt so frustrated that he spent a lot of time feeling sorry for him.

"Wait a minute!" Patrick finally said to himself. "This isn't helping my buddy at all, and I'm feeling lousy too. What can I do to help?"

Patrick began changing his thoughts about Jed. He remembered that positive thoughts are like prayers, and he certainly wanted to help Jed. So each time Patrick began to worry or feel sorry for his friend, he said to himself, "Stop!" Then he began to picture Jed safe and happy. Since changing his thoughts about Jed, Patrick feels a lot better about him.

Positive thought: Worrying about friends does not help them. I can best help my friends by thinking good thoughts about them.

The Middle-School Scaries

"I'm a little afraid to go to middle school next year," Bess told her dad as she helped him cook the dinner. "In fact, I don't even want to go on the tour of the school tomorrow," she continued.

"Part of your concern is that you don't know what middle school is like," her dad said. "When you get more information, I don't think you'll be so nervous."

"That's the problem," Bess said. "I *do* have information. I hear we have forty seconds between classes and that the older kids stuff the sixth graders in lockers on Fridays!"

"Sounds like some of the 'facts' you have heard may be fiction," her dad laughed. "That just adds to the middle-school scaries."

Bess wrinkled her forehead and thought for a minute. "I'm going to call Alison and get her to help me come up with a list of questions we can ask on the school tour tomorrow," she said.

At school the next day, Bess learned that she had four *minutes,* not forty seconds, between classes. And she didn't meet anyone who'd spent a Friday inside a locker!

Positive thought: Finding out correct information about new situations puts my mind at ease.

Being Liked

When Ray gave his campaign speech to his fifth-grade class, the other kids' reactions surprised him. When he said the school should have a study period, some kids waved their flags and cheered. But others booed the idea.

The same mixed reactions happened when he suggested that the school sell more than just candy in the snack machines.

Afterwards, a teacher noticed that Ray seemed upset. They talked about it.

"If I'm elected, how am I going to make everybody happy?" Ray asked. "I'd like everybody to like me. But how will they, when one person wants one thing and another wants something totally different?"

"Ray, you *can't* please everybody," his teacher said. "If you try, you will be like an animal chasing its tail—you'll never get anywhere, just dizzy.

"The only way not to offend anybody in your campaign is just to keep your mouth shut. And *then* you'd bother someone else for being a wimp!"

Ray grinned. That's how he thought of the other candidate, who hadn't said much of anything in his speech.

Positive thought: I do what I think is right. If others like me, great. If not, I still like myself.

I Can Cope with This!

The neighbors were really making a racket: screaming, hooting, and hollering. Beth was trying to relax and read, and the noise made her mad. She was about to work herself into a fit about it when she remembered that today was the day she had planned not to worry about anything for the whole day.

She needed to turn her emotions around from worrying and stewing about neighborhood noise to relaxing. To do this, she invented a mental game. She called it the "I can cope" game.

She compared her immediate peeve with five or six imaginary, clearly worse, problems. Then she asked herself, "I could have all these problems. Instead I have mine. Can't I cope with this one?" The answer was a loud "Yes."

A funny thing happened. Throughout the afternoon when she heard the neighbor's loud play, she grinned and said to herself, "I can cope with this." She could, in fact, and felt stronger for it.

Positive thought: I feel proud that I can cope with things.

Have Your Cake and Eat It Too

While his parents were at a workshop, Jamie spent the afternoon with his friend Ron. After the workshop, Jamie's parents called to see if he wanted to go out to eat with them or stay and play at Ron's house. They told him that Perry Unger, his parents' close friend, was having dinner with them.

"What a decision!" Jamie said. "Perry is my favorite adult friend. I'd love to eat with him. But Ron's soccer team won the championship this afternoon, and they invited me to have pizza with the team." After a brief silence, Jamie said, "I have an idea. Why don't we invite Perry over for dessert, and I can visit with him then?"

Everyone thought that was a great idea.

Jamie enjoyed the pizza party that afternoon. Later that evening, Jamie visited with Perry. As they ate their coconut cake, Perry winked at Jamie and said, "I guess you *can* have your cake and eat it too."

Positive thought: I can have more than one good thing.

Thinking About God

One cool spring evening, little John snuggled up beside Grandpa in the big blue double rocking chair. They rocked and talked, and talked and rocked.

"Pops?" John asked. "What did you think about God when you were my age?"

Grandpa rubbed his beard as he rocked. "Well," he said. "I thought God was a great big old man up in the sky who looked a lot like I do now. He had a long white beard."

"But what else did you think about God?" John persisted.

"I was taught that God is love. But I also got the idea somewhere that God watched everything I did. I was afraid that one day I'd do something bad enough that God might zap me.

"You might say I was a little confused about God then," Grandpa said, smiling. John burst out laughing.

"What do *you* think about God?" asked Grandpa.

"God is all the love I can think of—Mom's, Dad's, my friends', all our relatives'. All of it is mixed up together and then more love is added. That's what I think about God. God is love," John said.

Grandpa put his arm around John as they rocked and talked until the moon came up.

Positive thought: God is love. God expresses love through me and through all the people in my life.

Thinking About God

The Worrywart's Pledge

Emily was a worrywart. When a friend asked her to play and she didn't want to, she worried that saying so would hurt her friend's feelings. She worried about what other people thought of her. She worried about things she had said—even compliments.

All this worrying *hurt*. Emily sometimes lay awake late at night reviewing things that had happened that day. She would "second-guess" what people said to her, worrying that there was a second meaning behind their remarks. Emily was miserable.

When she was thoroughly sick of her misery, Emily made up the "Worrywart Pledge of Allegiance." She stood in front of a mirror and looked straight at herself. "I do the best I can," she said. "If it's my best, then it's good enough for everyone. People like me and what I say and what I do." Then she smiled at herself.

Emily repeated this pledge every morning and night. Before long, her worrywart days were over.

Positive thought: I can control my worrying. It's just a habit that a neat kid like me can handle once I learn how to.

The Worry-Free Way

All the way home, Connie listened to her friend Jessica talk about her bad day. Jessica had not been chosen for chorus. And she was having a lot of trouble with math. Connie let her friend talk and talk.

When she got home, Connie said to her mom, "Mother, you know how a good friend listens to her friends? Well, after you listen to sad stuff, it kind of makes you sad too, you know? I almost feel I'm supposed to feel sad all night because Jessica feels sad."

"I know exactly what you mean!" said Mom. "Every night I watch the news on TV, and so much of it is sad: about war, about crime. Sometimes I feel that I'm getting a message: 'Be a good citizen—worry!'"

But worrying doesn't help the world any more than it's helping Jessica or Connie. In fact, it hurts. It makes people feel bad. It magnifies fear by putting attention on what's wrong, not right.

Connie has done the best thing she can do for Jessica: just *be there* for her as a friend. True friendship is a much more powerful force than worry. And if everybody listened to each other as friends, the world might suffer less crime and war.

Positive thought: Worrying about my friends' troubles doesn't help them, and it hurts me. I can help by keeping them company and by listening.

Dad Might Lose His Job

Dad might lose his job. His boss called and told him so. Mike watched, but his dad did not seem very upset. In fact, Mike had not heard Dad even mention it much. He certainly didn't seem to be feeling sorry for himself about it. Mike decided to have a man-to-man talk with Dad about this.

"Are you worried?" he asked.

"You know, Mike, I was—but just for a moment. I felt fear tighten my throat when I got the phone call. But then a funny thing happened. As clear as a bell, a poem popped into my mind."

"A poem?" Mike asked. He could not imagine his dad reading any poetry, except maybe Shel Silverstein's.

Dad looked a little sheepish. "Yeah, well actually, it's more like what we used to call a ditty. It's really kind of corny. Except that after I heard it, I felt very calm, and I've been peaceful ever since. The funny thing is, I know I never read it anywhere, but I heard it as clearly as if somebody had recited it in my ear:

> I don't need sympathy
> I don't need fear
> I don't need a pity party
> God is here.

Positive thought: I can handle fear; God is here.

59

Worrisome Things

When Pete feels a little sad or out of sorts, he knows that something is bothering him. He goes off by himself for a few moments to a place where he can be very still and figures out exactly what it is. Perhaps he has hurt someone's feelings. Or someone has hurt him. Perhaps he's scared about something. In short, he is worried.

After he figures out what is worrying him, he takes the problem to God *right away*. God is the highest power in the universe. Nothing scares God. Then Pete waits until he feels calm settle over him, like a blanket when he's shivering. Then he says, "Thank you."

When Pete feels he needs to talk to someone, he does. If he needs to forgive someone (including himself), he does. And when this worry sticks up its ugly little head again, he gets tough with it. "God's taken care of you," he says. "I'm not thinking about you anymore." Then he goes on to other things.

Positive thought: If I'm worried, I figure out what's bothering me and turn it over to God. Then I do what I need to do!

What I Want to Be

Mr. Samuels found his nine-year-old daughter, Sarah, staring off into space, chewing on her pencil.

"What's up, Sarah?" he asked. "You're turning that pencil into a toothpick!"

"I just can't decide what I want to be when I grow up," Sarah sighed. "I want to be a teacher or a librarian. But I also want to be a gymnast and a mother besides. I can't stand having to choose."

"Why choose?" Dad said. "Your mom is a teacher. And she used to volunteer in your school library. She's also an athlete, and, obviously, she's a mother.

"Not only that," Mr. Samuels continued, "you can have many different jobs at different points in your life. I have a friend who was a librarian. Then she decided those same skills—having a good memory, being well organized—could combine with her love of music, and she became a disc jockey! She was one of the best, too! Then she had a great idea for a machine, and now she's on her way to being a fantastic business woman."

There's no need to limit yourself. You've got plenty of time to be what you want to be. And tons of opportunities. Have fun!

Positive thought: I can be what I want to be. I can do what I want to do.

Think Small

Six-year-old Matt stared at himself in the mirror. More than anything in the world, Matt wanted to be a soccer star. He could see the uniform. He could hear the roar of the crowd. The only thing he couldn't see in this daydream was how to get from here to there. He wondered how he could make his dream happen.

Matt remembered the funny saying that thinking big actually starts with thinking small—big dreams happen through many small steps.

At this point, Matt's dream seemed almost too big for him to imagine. So he tried to find a step toward his dream that he *could* imagine. He and Sam next door were already kicking a ball around the yard. When they were older and more skillful, he thought, they could play pickup games on Saturdays in the park. If they worked very hard, maybe they could join the neighborhood league and the high school team someday.

Matt's small steps now prepare him for taking bigger steps when he is older. Step by step and day by day, he can slowly make his dreams come true.

Positive thought: Big dreams start with small steps. I'm going to take one step today.

Your Secret Longing

Meg's mother was driving Meg and her friend Alicia to school one morning. The girls were talking about what they wanted to be when they grew up. "Do you ever daydream about things you'd like to do?" Meg asked Alicia.

"Sure," said Alicia. "People tell me all the time that with my black hair and blue eyes, I could be a model. I lie in bed at night imagining myself modeling gowns in Paris. But I could *never* do a thing like that. I'd die of stage fright!"

"I know," said Meg. "I'm good at making up stories. I dream of writing books, but you have to be famous to be a writer. Nothing like that could *ever* happen to me."

"You know," said Meg's mother, "maybe you can't make your dreams come true *this minute,* while you're kids. But you could look for ways to make your dreams happen someday."

A few weeks later, Alicia heard about an acting class at the children's theater. She knew that she would overcome her stage fright by learning to talk in front of people. Meg made friends with Wade, a classmate who also liked to write. Twice a week they got together after school and read their stories to one another.

Meg and Alicia had both found new ways to start making their dreams come true.

Positive thought: I can prepare myself for what I want to be.

The Rehearsal

Before a play is produced, the actors and actresses have what is called a "dress rehearsal." Everyone dresses in costume and wears makeup exactly as if it were opening night. The curtain goes up and the actors put on the play, usually before a live audience of friends. This experience prepares the cast for the real thing.

Rehearsing can help anyone accomplish his or her goals. It is another small step to success. Eleven-year-old Kappy worked out an important problem by playing a "life rehearsal." She had been spending every waking moment thinking about Chuck, a boy in her class at school. If thinking about a person a lot meant that you liked him, then Kappy was in love.

Her problem was that whenever she was with him, she was totally tongue-tied. Her older sister Chris suggested rehearsals. "I'll pretend I'm Chuck, and you practice talking to me."

At first, Kappy felt embarrassed to death. She felt so stiff and fake. But after giggling and carrying on awhile, she started to be more natural. She just practiced smiling and saying "Hi, Chuck."

She practiced enough that one day at school the words just popped out. And the most wonderful thing happened. Chuck said "Hi" back!

Positive thought: I can make my dreams happen. I just have to take a step at a time.

Wildflowers

"Here's my favorite wildflower," Grandma said to Ryan. She pointed out several tiny, blushing white flowers with glossy leaves.

"It's called 'trailing arbutus.' It's the first flower out every spring. But I *never* pick them," she said.

"Why not?" Ryan asked.

"Because if you let them be, they spread," Grandma said. "Then we'll have more of them to enjoy. You know, some wildflowers have disappeared completely because people picked them all. It's sad."

Ryan thought so too. It didn't make sense to kill something beautiful just so you could look at it a little longer.

Positive thought: My respect is the gift I give back to nature to thank her for what she gives me.

What a Trophy Is—and Isn't

"This is my most exciting dance recital ever," Whitney said to her mom as she put on her costume. "I'll finally get a trophy."

At the recital Whitney danced exceptionally well. Then came time for the awards ceremony. Whitney beamed as she received her fifth-year trophy. Her mom and dad took lots of pictures.

The next morning she told her parents how much she loved the trophy and how she liked being recognized. But one thing puzzled her.

"I thought I would feel like a different person when I received the trophy," she said to her parents. "And I don't."

"That's because trophies are awarded to people for what they do. A trophy is not a measure of who they are," her mom replied. "You are much greater than any award you receive."

Positive thought: I am greater than any award I get—or don't get.

No Competition

Juan has never been able to master the back flip in gymnastics. He rarely makes the goals in soccer. He is inches taller than anybody else in his class, but in the other fourth-grade class there's a bigger girl. Math is hard for Juan, but he's a whiz at reading.

Juan has noticed that mentally and physically, people *aren't* all equal. Whatever he does, he always finds somebody else who can do it better and somebody who does it worse.

Except spiritually. Each person is a child of God. Each person expresses God in an original way. All God asks is that Juan be himself, something no one else can do.

Inside, nobody can be Juan's equal or even compare to him. Thinking of that, Juan feels safe and secure.

Positive thought: Being me is all God asks me to do. I cannot fail.

Fifty-Five Hundred Chances

Jane had been trying all day to get up the nerve to talk to the new gym teacher. Jane used to hate that class. Now she loved it. She felt it was important to tell her teacher that.

But she didn't. Once again, her shyness overcame her. Trying to be positive, she said to her dad that night, "Oh well, I guess I'll get a second chance."

Dad laughed. "Honey, you won't get just a second chance. Fifty-five hundred chances will come your way."

"What do you mean?" Jane asked.

"Life constantly gives you chances to try again, Jane," Dad said. "You never have to worry that you've blown it, that you've failed. Life will always give you another chance."

Positive thought: I get a lot of opportunities to succeed.

Finding the Music

"I'm just not going to band practice without my sheet music," said Marci. In ten minutes the school bus would pull up at her corner. Time was running out, and she felt frantic.

"I'll get a zero for the day, and I'll never be leader of the flute section. Oh, I'm always losing things," she cried with disgust as she plopped down on the sofa.

She tried to calm her mind. "All right, Marci," she said to herself. "Calm down a minute."

She took a couple of relaxing breaths and remembered when she last practiced her flute. She saw herself snap the case shut and carefully fold the music. Marci said to herself, "My mind knows where the music score is. I can find it."

Then she finished getting ready for school. While putting on her coat, thinking of something else, she suddenly remembered folding the music . . . and putting it on her desk, where she wouldn't forget it. Marci made it to the bus stop with time to spare.

"Whew!" she said when she climbed aboard the bus. "I couldn't find my music, and I was afraid I'd miss the bus!"

The driver laughed. "I'm late this morning because I couldn't find my keys!"

Positive thought: My mind likes helping me. I can tell it what I want, and it gives me what I need.

69

More Solutions Than You Can Dream Of

When James and Richard came home from school, they were both starving. Richard ran to the fruit bowl and grabbed the last piece of fruit—a big, ripe banana.

"Hey," said James. "I'm hungry too."

And the boys began to tug on the banana.

"Hold it, guys," said Ms. Murphy, the sitter. "If you keep that up, the banana will be so bruised nobody will eat it. You boys can figure out how to solve this without a fight."

James and Richard stared at each other for a minute, and then they thought of some solutions. Richard suggested they make a peanut butter and banana sandwich and split it. That would be enough for both of them. James thought they could share this banana while walking to the corner store to buy another one. They also looked in the cabinet for other snacks. There they found the perfect solution—a package of instant banana pudding. Soon they were eating the warm pudding with sliced banana on top.

Positive thought: I have many possibilities for solving problems. I use my mind to help me see them.

Asking for What You Want

"I'm learning how to say what I want, Mom," eight-year-old Terry said to his mother.

"Tell me about it," his mother said.

"Well, last year, whenever I was at Bob's house playing and his mom asked if I wanted something to drink, I always said I didn't know, even if I was really thirsty," Terry said. "Mrs. Bishop used to smile at that, so I started saying yes if Bob did," he continued.

"But now when Mrs. Bishop asks me if I'm thirsty and I am, I just say yes. I'm glad that I can say that now. I always felt a little silly saying I didn't know if I wanted a drink."

Terry feels good about asking for what he wants. What's more, he has a much better chance of getting it if he asks for it!

Positive thought: I can say what I want and don't want.

Hands in the Cement

When Tom was a child, his dad tore up the old, crumbling sidewalk to their house and put in a new one.

When the cement had just been poured into the wooden frames, Dad called Mom and Tom and his seven brothers and sisters together. "Let's put a memory of our family into the cement," he said.

So they did. Each of the children pressed a hand into the slimy roughness. They held it for a moment and then let go. There in the new sidewalk were ten handprints, ranging from the very tiny one of one-year-old David up to Dad's big palm. Once the cement dried, it was hard as a rock; and there were all of their prints, recorded forever in the cement. For the rest of their time in that house, they could marvel at the growth in their hands and their lives since the day Dad laid the sidewalk.

Positive thought: I like being a part of my family and celebrating it.

Hands in the Cement

Mind Pictures

Some friends invited John and Paul to a party at the amusement park.

John was excited. He had two weeks to earn money for the trip. His mom paid him for doing extra chores like cleaning the bathroom. He also earned money by cutting the neighbor's lawn. Each day he pictured the good time he would have riding rides, playing games, and eating popcorn and cotton candy.

Paul had a different set of pictures in his mind. He saw himself being bored and sitting at home. He complained that the amusement park was too expensive for him. He did nothing to prepare to go.

Two weeks passed. John went to the amusement park and had a great time. Paul sat at home and was bored.

Positive thought: I picture what I want—*not* what I don't want.

Positive Talk and Pictures

A lice and Jerry were discussing how they learn to do new activities.

"The way I learned to ride a skateboard," Jerry said, "was to watch the other kids and then picture myself doing what they did. The older boys' tricks showed me what I could do."

Alice nodded her head. "I talked to myself when I was learning to ride my bike uphill," she told Jerry. "I would say, 'I can do it, I can do it,' as I pedaled up the hill. I also tried to relax and enjoy it," she said.

These children were using the power of their minds to help them learn a new skill. They told themselves with pictures and words that they could succeed. And they did.

Positive thought: Positive talk and positive pictures help me learn to do new activities.

Vacuuming on a Summer's Day

Charlie practically stumbled over his friend Mac one day in the field behind his home. There Mac lay, on his back in the weeds, chewing a blade of grass.

"Mac," said Charlie. "I've been looking all over for you. What are you doing?"

"Vacuuming," said Mac.

Charlie looked sharply at Mac. "Whoa, buddy," he said. "You've flipped out now. What are you talking about?"

"I read that some people imagine they have a vacuum inside their body. They push it up and down their veins to get rid of germs or pain. But I was using the vacuum for other stuff."

"Like what?" asked Charlie.

"Like being mad at my sister this morning. And feeling bored sometimes in the summer. I'm just vacuuming around inside me to get rid of anything I don't want. It's kind of fun."

Charlie took a long look at Mac, and then flopped down beside him on the grass.

Positive thought: I can get rid of my unpleasant thoughts.

Mental Skiing

The children in the boat cheered as they drove by. Roy was up on the water skis.

"Looking good!" the children called out.

Earlier that afternoon, Roy had talked with Aunt Marie about waterskiing. He wanted more than anything to be able to ski around the lake this summer, but so far he hadn't been able to stand up for more than a few seconds.

"Try waterskiing in your mind!" said Aunt Marie.

First, Roy pictured himself putting on the skis. Then he heard the boat rev up its engine. He felt himself being pulled up and onto his feet. He came out of the water and glided along as if he had always known how. Several times he imagined this scene, feeling the wind in his face and the waves thumping under his skis.

Later, when Roy walked down to the lake to try waterskiing again, he knew he could do it. And now he was actually skiing around the lake—just as he had imagined.

Positive thought: My confidence builds as I see myself doing what I really want to do.

Different Kinds of Genius

The word *genius* usually describes two types of people: artists or those who are very smart.

In fact, there are many kinds of geniuses. Pat, who can get even the bossiest person to listen, is a genius at dealing with people.

Brady, who helps his friends feel comfortable discussing things, is a genius at being just himself with everyone. Or perhaps he has the genius of being a good listener. Other people flock to him.

Karen's shyness makes her companions feel witty and daring. Her gentleness is endearing. She has the gift of making others realize *their* gifts.

All of these people have a genius for appreciating others. Our world needs these people.

Positive thought: Today I think of the people in my life who appreciate me, listen to me, and overlook my mistakes. I learn from these people and appreciate them.

Sharing Feelings

F rank stayed after the Boy Scout meeting to talk with his troop leader.

"I can't believe my parents are adopting another child," he confided to Mr. Abbott. "They seem so excited, and I don't want to spoil it for them. So I've even been pretending I'm happy about it," he said. "But I wonder whether I'm not good enough for them."

Mr. Abbott was silent for a few minutes. But Frank felt better already, just expressing his feelings to someone.

"Your parents have lots of love to share," Mr. Abbott began. "One of the reasons they are adopting another child is to share this love. I have learned that when I give love, I seem to have more to give. I hope it will be the same with your parents.

"I wish you would talk to your parents about how you feel. They may not have a clue, especially since you've been pretending to be happy," Mr. Abbott said.

"Thanks for listening," Frank said. "I've been hiding these feelings from my parents for so long, I thought if I *did* say some-thing, I might explode. I think I can handle talking to them now, though."

Positive thought: Talking out my feelings helps. I always have someone I can share my feelings with.

Crying over Spilled Milk

On Friday night the Ropers always go out to dinner. They were having an unusually good time one evening until they heard a crash at the next table.

A little girl had knocked her milk over. You would have thought she had done something horrible. "You're so clumsy," her dad shouted. "Just look at the big mess you've made."

Tears ran down the child's face as she felt everybody's eyes on her. The restaurant became very quiet.

On the way home in the car, Mr. and Mrs. Roper talked to their son Ken about the girl.

"I wanted to go over to the table and give her a big hug when her dad was yelling at her," Mrs. Roper said.

"I did too," Ken said.

Then Mr. Roper told Ken something he had never mentioned before. He said that *his* parents used to yell at him that way. They used to say he couldn't do anything right.

"I finally learned to tell myself things that made me feel better," Ken's father said. "I would say silently, 'No matter what you say to me, I am still all right.' That always helped me feel better. That helped me take care of myself when I was a child."

Positive thought: No matter what anybody says to me, I am still all right.

The New Colt

M r. Martin bought a brand new colt for his daughters, Sarah and Tamara. They were both thrilled. Sarah had been taking riding lessons for a year. Having her own horse seemed like the best thing in the world.

At least she thought so until that afternoon. Then Sarah noticed that her parents were letting Tamara ride the horse more. And they were oohing and aahing over her.

Sarah was so jealous of the attention her parents gave Tamara that she forgot some things. Like the fact that Tamara was a lot younger and needed more of her parents' attention while riding. Sarah also forgot that she had already had a year of riding lessons, but her sister had never ridden before.

Finally Sarah got sick of being in a bad mood. One thing she did was to try to be happy for her sister by remembering *her* first day of riding. Then she decided to teach Tamara a few skills she had learned from her own lessons. When she saw Tamara's face light up, Sarah began to enjoy the afternoon too.

Positive thought: I can choose to enjoy whatever I am doing.

Making a Sandwich

Making a sandwich usually means putting mayonnaise on two pieces of bread and adding some meat, lettuce, and a slice of tomato.

At the Bradford house it means something different.

They make a *people* sandwich. Here is the recipe. They take two adults and one or two children. They put the adults together in a big hug. Then Suzy and Amy say, "Make a sandwich!" and they squeeze themselves between their parents for a big family hug.

This is one of the ways the Bradfords express love at home.

Positive thought: Today I express love at home.

What You Water Grows

Kay's neighbor, Mr. Holman, has the same kind of flowers in his yard as Kay does. Yet Mr. Holman's are gorgeous, full of many blooms. Kay's are a bit scraggly—actually, they're pretty pitiful.

So Kay asked him, "What do you do?"

"I feed them," Mr. Holman said. "I put fertilizer in water and I feed them."

Pretty simple. But the answer had not been obvious to Kay, who didn't know you have to feed outdoor flowers often.

Now Kay knows that flowers are just like everything else: they flourish when you feed them. Loving attention improves everything—whether it is flowers or tennis skills or friendship.

Positive thought: Like every living thing, I grow when I am fed. And giving my attention to something I care about is how I feed it.

Feeling Blue

Ten-year-old Sam was bored and blue. School had been out only four weeks, and already the summer seemed endless, like the Montana prairie Sam viewed from his window.

At breakfast one morning, Dad said, "According to the newspaper, homeless people are suffering a lot of problems here. People have lost their jobs and then their homes and apartments. Now whole families are without food and places to stay."

Sam imagined how he would feel if he didn't have a bed or supper. It bothered him so much that instead of thinking about his boredom, he started thinking about the homeless people's troubles. He asked his mom whether she thought a kid could do anything to help.

"Why not?" Mom said. "It certainly wouldn't hurt to try." Together, they made a list of places he could call to offer his help. On his third call, he found a church that served meals every day. They needed somebody to help clear tables.

Sam took the volunteer job. Twice a week, his dad dropped him off on his way to work. Sam liked the responsibility and he liked the people. He liked knowing that he was helping someone else.

And one day he noticed that he wasn't bored anymore.

Positive thought: One cure for sadness and boredom is doing something for someone else.

A Personal Celebration

Every Fourth of July at Lake Burton, where Andy and his family live, people fire off brilliant rockets. All day, boats speed by and firecrackers pop and echo across the lake. During a rare quiet moment, Andy stands on the deck of his home, gazing at the water and the mountains. He enjoys the stillness.

In his own quiet way, Andy is also celebrating America's birthday. He celebrates his country by enjoying its beauty. Not all celebrations are noisy. Some are just between friends. Some are just inside ourselves. And some, like Andy's, are just between people and nature.

Positive thought: There are many moods in my life. I enjoy the quiet times, as well as the "party times."

Fat Cat and Linda's Dad

L inda looked out her bedroom window. There at the far end of the backyard was her dad, sitting in the big outdoor lounge chair. Her fat gray cat, Smokey, was curled up in Dad's lap. They both looked perfectly content.

Linda was startled by this glimpse of a new side of Dad's personality. When other people were watching, he never said a kind word about Smokey. He always called her "a useless animal." Once he even threatened to give her away because she bothered his rabbits. So it did seem a little strange to see the cat cuddled up in his lap. Dad was even petting her!

"Why can't Dad be nice like that in front of people?" Linda wondered. "Maybe he thinks it's silly to love an animal."

Whatever the reason, Linda enjoyed seeing a new side of her father.

Positive thought: People are complicated. By noticing the little things they do, I can learn about the people I love.

Playing Barbie Dolls

Greta Harmon's mom was a part-time everything: student, homemaker, and secretary. Going to school and working didn't leave her much time to spend with her family. Greta didn't like it.

One Saturday, when she thought Mom might have time, Greta practically begged her to play Barbie dolls.

"Play isn't on my busy schedule," said Mom, "but I guess I could take a little time for that."

They dressed the Barbie dolls in shimmering evening gowns and had a fashion show. Mom seemed to forget how busy she was as she got lost in the world of tiny clothes. At bedtime, Mom said, "I really enjoyed playing with you. The funny thing is that I did all the chores I had planned for today, even though I took time out to play." She smiled. "Maybe I worked so well *because* I took time out!"

Positive thought: Taking time to play is important.

Getting There

While Harry and his dad were walking on the beach, the heaviest rainstorm of their lives struck suddenly.

"How can we get home?" Harry asked his dad. "It's raining so hard that the road has disappeared. I'm scared."

"I know we can get through this, Harry," Dad said. "Although we can't see the road from here, we know it is there, and we know we will get to it. We'll reach it by moving forward and taking one step at a time."

Later when they were wrapped in blankets, eating hot soup Mom had made for them, Harry said, "For a while this afternoon I wasn't sure we would make it home. I felt like giving up."

"Well I'm glad you decided to take a few more steps," Dad said.

Positive thought: I continue moving toward my goals and I get there—one step at a time.

Top-Bunk Cooperation

All the top bunks were taken when five-year-old Maria arrived at camp. That was fine with her because sleeping on a lower bunk seemed safer.

During rest time, though, Maria eyed the top bunks. Being up high in the room did look like fun.

A couple of the older girls noticed Maria's curiosity about the top bunks. "Here's an idea," said Tanya. "Let's push all the beds together and let Maria sleep in the middle. That way she won't fall off."

The other girls agreed. The beds were lined up from wall to wall—full of girls! Maria slept right in the middle—safe and sound.

Positive thought: Cooperation helps everyone have what he or she wants. Today I cooperate.

Homesick

All the girls in the cabin could hear the quiet sobs from the bunk in the corner. Maryann was homesick and unable to fall asleep on her first night at camp.

Sally Jordan, the camp counselor, stood beside Maryann's bed and rubbed her back. She talked quietly to Maryann. "Tell me about your room at home and the toys you like to sleep with."

"A teddy bear named Bill," said Maryann, still snuffling, hardly able to talk.

Sally rolled up a shirt and tucked it into Maryann's arm. "Close your eyes now, and pretend that this is Bill, and you're in your own bed at home. Imagine that you're comfortable and safe in your own room. Your parents are sleeping right across the hall."

The sobbing began to get softer. Maryann began to relax. Soon she fell into a peaceful sleep.

Positive thought: When I create a safe feeling in my mind, I am no longer afraid.

A Fish Story

The bass boats are trolling past Vince's anchored boat on the green waters of Lake Burton. There's a mist rising from the lake. The sun has just risen.

Vince sits silently for hours, knowing that this lake isn't very good for fishing but enjoying the sunlight on the water and the sight of ducks nibbling at the water for food. Suddenly, a fish bites. Vince and the fish fight it out. The fish is pulling hard, causing the rod to arch close to the water. His heart pounding, Vince is pulling too, just as hard. As he brings him alongside the boat, the fish leaps, throws the hook, and swims away.

Vince feels disappointed, but he hasn't spent hours for only a minute's excitement in catching a fish. Now he puts his rod away and raises the anchor. He trails his hand in the water, letting the boat drift toward shore.

Positive thought: It's okay just to want some peace and quiet. No excuses are necessary.

I Think I Can!

It was an exciting summer for Brent because he had been chosen to work as an assistant at day camp. He was in charge of story time once a week.

Brent had just turned twelve. Ever since he was a little boy, he had been taught the power of positive thinking. He was looking forward to teaching the younger children some of the ideas he loved so much. He planned his first story time around his very favorite story, *The Little Engine That Could,* the story about a little train that was able to pull a big load up a hill by saying, "I think I can. I think I can."

After the story hour, the children lined up and pretended they were the little train. "I think I can. I think I can," they repeated as they choo-chooed around the classroom.

Brent was pleased with his first story time. When the camp director asked him whether he thought he could do as well the next week, Brent had an answer ready.

Positive thought: When I think I can, I can!

Cleaning Closets

Ellen and her older sister Alyssa spent one Saturday cleaning out their closet. Some of their clothes no longer fit. When Ellen tried to squeeze into her favorite jeans, for example, there was just no way to do it comfortably. Not only did she look silly with her jeans high above her ankles, but she also felt awful because she could hardly breathe!

"Time to give those away," Alyssa said to her sister.

"But they're my favorite jeans!" Ellen protested.

Alyssa suggested that Ellen look in the mirror. When she did, both girls burst out laughing. Ellen couldn't take off the jeans quickly enough when she saw how ridiculous they looked. She tossed them in the box for the Salvation Army.

Experience will teach Alyssa and Ellen that their minds are like closets too—mental storehouses. One day they'll find that a few of their old ideas like "I'm stupid" or "I can't handle this" just don't "fit" anymore.

The girls can fill their minds with more useful thoughts like "I feel good about myself," "I get along with others," and "I am in control of my life."

Positive thought: I replace negative ideas about myself with positive thoughts.

Unpleasant Chores

Saturday morning is the time when Jeff and his dad clean house. Some chores are just plain gross to Jeff—like cleaning the bathroom. One day, he was complaining noisily about it.

"Jeff," Dad said, "Can you think of any way to make this job more pleasant?"

"The only way I could make it more pleasant is to watch someone else do it," Jeff replied.

"You're spending about fifty-two hours a year in a grumpy mood because of your attitude about this chore." said Dad. "You do have a choice in the matter."

Jeff smiled as he imagined a maid coming to do this chore for him. But he quickly came back to reality. A maid was *not* the kind of choice Dad meant.

The wheels of Jeff's mind began to turn.

"Maybe if I put on some loud music, I'll be in a better mood," he said.

"I'll bet that will help me too while I mop the kitchen floor," Dad said.

It *did* help both of them. In no time at all, they were singing as they worked. The name of the song was "I've Got a New Attitude."

Positive thought: I can find a way to make unpleasant things more pleasant.

The Neighborhood Club

The children in the neighborhood have formed a club. They have a secret handshake. And a secret name.

Actually, this is not the first time they've tried to form a club. The first one fell apart after two days because everybody wanted to be president. When it became clear that everybody couldn't, they all stuck out their bottom lip and went home.

Now it's a month later, and the excitement of a secret club has bubbled to the surface once more. So they're trying again. They've solved the president problem: they're taking turns.

This time, they're fighting over who gets to be secretary. Someone's father gave them an old appointment calendar. Everyone suddenly realized how much fun writing down minutes in the official-looking, leather-like book would be.

In fact, the biggest fight happened when the president quit because *she* wanted to be the secretary and then wasn't chosen for the job. So once again, there have been some hard feelings.

But this time, they didn't all go home mad. This time, they wanted the club so much that they worked things out.

Positive thought: Being a part of a group is fun. And it teaches me how to work out problems and get along with other people.

The Blame Game

M r. Logan slammed on his brakes as he rounded the corner. A young boy had fallen near the street.

The boy jumped up, and Mr. Logan could hear him yelling at his friends.

"You idiots," he screamed. "See what you made me do. You almost pushed me in front of that car. You make me so mad!"

The boy had been playing tag in the yard with his friends. One of them accidentally tripped him, and he rolled to the curb.

But the boy was playing another game besides tag. He was playing "the blame game." He blamed his fall on someone else because he was scared and shaken for a moment and wanted someone else to take responsibility for what had happened.

When he says that other people are "making him mad," he is really taking his anger out on them. Learning to accept feelings can be hard sometimes. But it's more honest for him to accept them than to blame someone else.

Positive thought: I am truthful about my feelings.

Problems, Problems

"Dad, I think I'm doing something wrong," eleven-year-old Blake confided. "No matter how hard I try, it seems I'm always facing some problem."

"You feel that once you get your act together, you won't have any problems—is that it, Son?" Dad asked. Blake nodded.

Dad smiled. "Blake, I was in my mid-twenties before I realized that problems were not a sign that I was doing something wrong—they are just a part of life."

Blake's face fell. A lifetime of problems—yikes! But at the same time, he felt a little relieved. He had worked so hard to avoid problems that it was kind of a relief to find out that having them was normal.

"One good thing," Dad said, "is that if problems are an everyday occurrence, then being able to solve them must be too. Meeting hurdles and overcoming them must be part of being a boy or girl, man or woman."

Positive thought: My problems are opportunities to grow.

Listening for Answers

Peace of mind means being happy with your life.

When parts of their life are making them unhappy, many people find peace of mind by asking God, their Higher Power, for help with problems. They pray about whatever bothers them most. It doesn't matter if someone else would think it was silly. A small stone in your sneaker can drive you nuts. The same is true of small, nagging problems.

These people pray about their problems, one at a time, asking God to help them figure out exactly what's wrong. They let God know they're ready to solve the problem. Then they listen and look for answers.

Sometimes the problem disappears. Sometimes it doesn't, but their attitude toward it changes, so it isn't bothersome anymore. This change is also an answer to a prayer.

Positive thought: I take my problems to God. I ask to know what to do about them.

An Inside Job

Scott and his mom ran out to greet Rodney and help him bring his luggage into the house. Rodney was grinning from ear to ear. He was so happy to see his friend. He hadn't seen Scott since he moved away last summer! On Rodney's shirt was a big purple button with yellow letters that said "Smile and be happy."

"That's certainly appropriate," Scott's mother thought as she looked at Rodney's button. "He's one of the happiest kids I've ever seen."

During dinner, the family asked Rodney how he liked living in a different town. They wanted to know about his new friends and his new school.

"You seem happy most of the time," Mom said to Rodney. "What kinds of things make you happy?"

"Oh, visiting friends, going swimming, and playing," he replied. He paused for a minute as he was trying to think of more things. Then he said, "I really don't know what makes me happy. I'm just happy most of the time. It's more of a feeling I have inside than something going on outside myself that makes me happy."

"Sounds like happiness is an inside job with you!" Mom said.

Positive thought: I am happy from the inside out.

Moving

When Phil's parents told him on Saturday that they were going to move to the mountains, he was still for a minute. He felt kind of wooden inside. It seemed he heard every single sound in the room. Then, slowly, he realized exactly what moving would mean. More time to fish. More walks with his dad. Even being able to eat and drink in the den at the cabin, unlike at home in the city, where Mom had a fit about his spilling things on the carpet.

"I like the idea," he said at last.

So why was he lying in bed on Sunday feeling scared and confused? One reason was that it was going to be hard to tell his friends. If he acted excited about the move, would they think he didn't like them and found it easy to leave?

"That's not true at all," Phil said to himself as tears formed in his eyes. "I am really going to miss my friends and my life here."

Phil lay back on the bed and cried and cried until no more tears would come. Then he fell asleep.

Positive thought: Tears help us deal with sad things, like good-byes. Tears can wash away pain.

Wrapped in Love

"Hurry, hurry," the Kelly girls called as the Newbergs pulled to a stop in front of the Kelly cabin. "Can we give Tara her present now?" they begged Mrs. Kelly.

"At least wait until they get out of the car," Mrs. Kelly laughed.

Mrs. Newberg came into the house first. The girls pulled her into their bedroom to show what they had bought for her daughter. Hidden behind the bed was a beautiful doll. It had long blond hair and a bright satin costume.

"We're sorry it isn't wrapped," the girls said. They didn't have any wrapping paper at the cabin.

"But your gift *is* wrapped," Mrs. Newberg said. "You girls have wrapped it with love and joy."

When they gave the doll to Tara, it was hard to tell who was more excited—the Kelly girls or Tara!

Positive thought: Giving makes me happy.

Where Do You Pray?

"When I lived in Alaska," Mrs. Smith said, "I never went to church. I just went outside to pray. It was so beautiful that sometimes I just wanted to hug the earth. I've never felt closer to God."

Mrs. Smith's children go to church, and they like it. They learn a lot there. But still she likes to tell them this story because it shows that God is in more places than just church. One of the places where people feel closest to God is in nature.

Most people feel wonder when they see mountains or the ocean. But they can love the bark-rough climb up an apple tree too, or feel peace listening to the wind brushing through pine needles. Or thrill at the slow, majestic swish of a large bass's tail as it glides under the dock, or be awed by the beauty of a rainbow.

Mrs. Smith is not alone in seeing nature as God's church.

Positive thought: I am happy in the outdoors. I like seeing other creatures. I like rainbows and water and mountains.

Rich in Attitude

An elderly woman walked slowly through her garden. She snapped beans off the vines and dropped them into her apron, which she held like a basket in front of her. She stopped in front of her flower garden, letting her eyes feast on the sight, and letting the aroma of her favorite flowers float about her.

Anyone who saw this woman—old, bent over, dressed in drab gray woolens—might not think, "Now there's a rich woman." But she is doing what she wants, when she wants. She's rich. And she knows it!

"Rich" doesn't mean only money. A word for wealth existed before money was even invented! Rich is an attitude. People with no money at all can be rich.

Positive thought: I enjoy the things I do, and do the things I enjoy. How I "spend" my life and my time, and who I "spend" it with will help determine how "rich" my life is.

Bumps on the Head

Eleven-year-old Donna had been acting very bossy, especially to her brother Ben. In fact, her bossiness was putting a damper on the family's walking tour of New Orleans—until something stopped her.

"Watch out for that hole in the sidewalk!" Donna yelled at her brother. "It's a wonder you haven't fallen in one," she continued. "Look where you're . . ." Donna was stopped mid-sentence—she had bumped head-on into a streetlight!

A little stunned and embarrassed, but a whole lot nicer and quieter, Donna continued on the tour.

That evening, she laughed with her family about the incident. "This story would make a good fable," she said. "The moral would be, 'She who watches her own steps, and not her brother's, moves forward.'"

Positive thought: I pay attention to where I am going so I can move forward.

An Intelligent Place to Live

John and his dad were fascinated watching the big spider build her web in a bush in the backyard.

"How does it know which strands to put the sticky stuff on and which ones not to?" John asked his Dad. "And then how does it know not to step on the ones that are sticky?" he continued.

"All animals have an intelligence that helps them know how to do whatever they need to do," Dad said. "The intelligence that helps the spider stay off the sticky strands is similar to the intelligence that guides birds to fly south in the winter and causes animals to grow thicker fur for cold weather. The intelligence in a seed lets it know whether to grow into a watermelon or a tomato."

"I always knew I had intelligence inside me to help me know how to do things," John said. "But I never thought about animals and plants having intelligence too. I like the idea that there is intelligence all around me—in plants, animals, everything."

Positive thought: My world is full of intelligence.

An Intelligent Place to Live

Get It Out to Get It Over

"Ouch!" Todd yelled as he stubbed his toe on the back door. He limped over to Grandma to get a big hug.

"Did you see what happened?" Todd asked, and then told her before she even had a chance to answer.

But Grandma didn't interrupt Todd—even though she had seen what happened. She knew that if he kept his feelings inside, he'd have hurt feelings as well as a hurt toe.

A little later, Grandma asked Todd how his toe was. He looked at her questioningly. He had forgotten all about it.

Positive thought: I get out what is painful so I can get over it.

Celebrating with Our Friends

The Thompsons had left work early on Friday so they could see their friend Brian play the piano in a recital. The four-hour drive passed quickly as the family enjoyed the beautiful ride on country roads.

Ten-year-old Claire was especially pleased to be able to go because Brian had been her classmate in music before he moved to another town. She liked him very much and couldn't wait to see him and hear him play his recital piece.

"I feel so good today," she told her parents. "I really like sharing in the good things that happen to my friends."

Claire had learned to share her friends' happiness. When she saw Brian, she told him how glad she felt about his accomplishment. She didn't try to top it with a story about her own recital, but instead supported his moment of joy.

Positive thought: I enjoy sharing in the good things that happen to my friends.

The Birthday Party

"I really wish you would invite Mitch to your birthday party," Ms. Baker told her son Joshua. "His mother is a friend of mine, and I think it would be polite to invite him. You used to like him when you were younger," she continued.

"I don't like him at all now, and I don't want him to come," Joshua said. "Trust me, Mom," he said. "Mitch doesn't like me either. And he sure doesn't like my friends. It's a mutual feeling."

Ms. Baker thought about how she had raised Joshua to be honest. "I taught him to be honest in his feelings and actions. But now I want him to act as if he liked someone he really doesn't," she thought. "That's not really truthful."

The two continued their discussion. Ms. Baker told Josh that her parents had taught her she should like everybody.

"I tried and tried to like everybody as a kid. I always pretended that I did, even when I didn't. I faked it, and it didn't feel good," she told him.

"I also felt guilty if I didn't like someone," she said. "I just realized today that I was trying to force you to act as I did when I was a child. I'm sorry, Josh. You don't have to invite Mitch to the party. It's much more important to be honest. And if Mitch feels that way about you, he won't care anyway."

Positive thought: I am honest in my feelings and actions.

Disagreeing with Friends

Bonnie and George had an argument. It was not a *bad* fight, as fights go. Neither one insulted the other or said anything mean. Still, Bonnie felt uncomfortable.

George called Bonnie a little while later. His voice was very kind. "Let's talk about this some more."

Then Bonnie realized what had been missing from their argument. She was not sure she had let George know that no matter how much they disagreed, she still liked him. She had also been uncertain he would still like her after she disagreed with something he said.

It's okay for friends to disagree. Different people sometimes have different opinions. That's okay.

Positive thought: I can disagree with people and still be their friend.

The Wet Head

B etty invited her friend Dee over to spend the night. When it came time to take their showers, Betty debated about whether to wash her hair.

"My sister says if you go to sleep with your hair wet, you will catch cold," Dee said to Betty. "I even did it one night just to see if it was true, and sure enough, I woke up the next morning with a cold."

"That doesn't prove anything," Betty said, "because believing something will happen can make it happen. I've gone to sleep with wet hair dozens of times and never caught a cold from it."

If you've heard something over and over again, chances are you believe it. Your belief can make it true in your life. But you don't have to believe everything you hear!

Positive thought: My beliefs affect what happens in my life. I can change my beliefs if I want to.

What I Am

The twins were cooped up in the den all morning. Their parents had no idea what the girls were doing. All the parents knew was that the girls' project required scissors, glue, construction paper, magazines, and markers.

Just before lunch, the twins came out and proudly displayed their artwork. They each had a colorful collage made up of magazine headlines and photos. The title of each began with "I AM."

Pasted across the top of Anita's paper were the words "I AM A MAGNIFICENT MASTERPIECE." Her collage was filled with pictures of children from all over the world.

Deborah's poster was called "I AM A RAINBOW." She had pasted and drawn colorful rainbows all over her sheet. On the bottom of the page, she had written this little poem:

> Rainbows are beautiful
> Rainbows are fun
> They are so colorful
> I'm glad I'm one.

Dad smiled as he said to Mom, "They are as different as their posters, but one thing is for sure—they know they are wonderful."

Positive thought: I know I am wonderful.

The Sand Sculpture

Ms. Mueller stared at the sand sculpture in the wastebasket in the bathroom. The glass was broken and all the water had come out. Colored sand oozed through the cracked glass.

Guests had been visiting the Muellers for the past week. Their four rowdy cousins had just left this morning.

"One of them probably did it," Ms. Mueller thought.

She called her son Blaine into the bathroom, thinking he might know what happened.

Blaine looked at her sadly because he knew how fond she was of the sculpture.

"I did it, Mom," he said. "The boys and I brought it upstairs. They left it on the floor, and I stepped on it accidentally. I was waiting until they left to tell you about it."

Although Ms. Mueller talked sternly to Blaine for taking her treasure upstairs in the first place, she also told him how much his honesty meant to her. Blaine had to pay for the sculpture, but he was still glad that he had told the truth.

Positive thought: Being truthful is important to me.

The Assembly

Today was the first school assembly of the new school year. The children filed in and sat with their legs crossed on the floor. The kindergartners—who came first—sang songs while the other children walked in. One song had a surprise: the children had written in a line about their principal. When he heard it and looked up, surprised, the children all laughed.

Then came the program. First the principal introduced the school guards and thanked them for helping the children cross the streets in the morning.

Then a third grader sang a song that she had written about the school. You could hear a pin drop when she sang it in her high, soft voice. Soon kids were humming along. When she finished, everybody clapped.

Finally, the principal held up the framed artwork of two children. They had drawn the pictures themselves over the summer and gave them to the school as presents. The principal promised to hang them in the school hall.

The assembly was over. For half an hour the children had heard only good news about themselves, their school, and each other. What a wonderful reason for an assembly!

Positive thought: Everywhere there are people who notice and applaud the good things in life. I'm one of those people.

Uncle Bill's Problem

One night Uncle Bill drove up unexpectedly to the house. Randy, playing at the neighbor's, dropped everything to run and greet him. Uncle Bill was his favorite relative.

Soon after, settled in the den, Uncle Bill told Randy that he had been in the hospital. He had gone there to stop drinking.

Nine-year-old Randy was shocked. *"You,* Uncle Billy? *You're* an alcoholic? Randy had always imagined that people with alcohol and other drug problems were different from other people.

As he listened to his uncle talk about his treatment, Randy felt many different emotions churning inside him. One was confusion. He had always thought Uncle Bill had the world by the tail.

And he also felt pride because his uncle thought Randy was grown-up enough to know the truth.

Finally, he felt sadness settle over him. "I'm sorry that I never guessed what was the matter," Randy said. "I should have known. I should have helped you."

"Hold it, Randy," said Uncle Bill. "Nobody could read my mind or run my life but me. Seeing what a great kid you are has always meant a lot to me—it's one of the reasons I wanted to be sober again. So you helped me, just by being you."

Positive thought: The greatest gift I can give others is to be myself.

113

The Snake

Rachel White and her mother worked out a deal to trade housekeeping jobs. Rachel agreed to clean the living room and kitchen, while her mother did the upstairs bedrooms.

Rachel cleaned busily. She was almost done when she went upstairs and asked her mom to trade back to their usual chores.

"What's going on?" her mom asked. "You're almost finished, and I still have lots more to do."

"I saw a snake on the kitchen floor, and I don't want to be in the same room with it," Rachel blurted out.

Mom figured that their cat had brought in a "present" from the woods. She went downstairs with Rachel to take care of the situation.

She went over to the small brown object on the floor. Then she just leaned over and picked it up! Rachel turned white with fear.

But what her mom had in her hand was not a snake at all. It was a clipping off the Swedish ivy plant. This brown, slightly curved object looked just like a little garter snake.

When Rachel realized what it was, she laughed and laughed. She was no longer afraid. She took the "snake" outside to scare her father with it.

Positive thought: When I take a closer look at what I fear, I may find it's not scary at all.

Taking Chances

Every day when Dad dropped off his five-year-old son at the nursery school, it was all he could do to leave. Brad always hung onto his pant leg and begged his dad not to leave.

But when Mom came to pick Brad up in the afternoon, he didn't want to go home. He hid so he could play some more with his friends.

One day, Brad's parents decided to talk with him about this. "How come you never want to stay in the morning, but we can't get you to leave in the afternoon?" Dad asked.

Brad thought a moment and said, "In the morning I feel shy. But during the day, the shy washes away."

What happened to Brad happens to all of us. We get shy about trying new things. But we find that when we go ahead and try them, the shyness wears off, and we enjoy having something new in our life.

Positive thought: Sometimes I feel shy. That's okay. But I'm not going to let it stop me from having fun.

The Steps I Take

Darlene was glad that September had come because dance class started again. Practicing every day and spending two hours in class each week didn't bother her at all. She loved to dance.

At dinner before class, Darlene was talking with her mom.

"I'm so excited," she said. "We get to start learning our recital numbers tonight."

"Isn't this a little early?" Mom asked. "Recital isn't until June. I think I'd get bored going over the same dances for nine months getting ready for one important night."

"I never get tired of dancing," Darlene answered. "And besides, getting ready for recital is just as much fun as the recital itself. I like it every step of the way."

Positive thought: I enjoy all the steps I take to reach my goals.

The First-Day-of-School Blues

Third-grader Angela was nervous, with a capital "N." She had just finished her first day of school, and everything had gone wrong. Her two best friends, Carrie and Bernadette, weren't in her class. And she hadn't gotten the teacher she wanted. Even worse, a couple of fourth graders on the bus told Angela that her teacher gave really hard homework every night.

"This year's going to be just awful," she said to her dad that night.

"Angela, I want to try an experiment with you," Dad said. "Here's a piece of paper. I want you to draw several clouds on it. Put a different thought about school in each cloud."

Angela had so much to write that her hand started to cramp up. "I'm scared," she wrote. "School isn't fun anymore." "My teacher gives too much homework." "I don't know anybody in my class." On and on she wrote.

When Dad saw Angela's paper, he said, "I'm not surprised you're scared and sad. Look at what you're telling yourself."

Looking at her list, Angela said, "Everything I wrote about school is bad."

"Bingo," said Dad. "When you tell yourself scary thoughts, guess what? You get scared."

"You know, I hardly knew anybody in my class the first day of school last year either. And now Carrie and Bernadette are my best friends," Angela said. "And those boys on the bus who said my teacher gives too much homework are *always* in trouble. I bet they never even *do* their homework."

Looking at her father, she said, "I feel better already, Dad. I got so worried I forgot how much I've always liked school."

Positive thought: How I talk to myself affects how I feel.

Why Pencils Have Erasers

"Why do pencils have erasers?" Dad asked Adam.
"To erase," he said.

"Erase what?" Dad pursued.

"Erase what you don't want . . . you know, your mistakes," Adam said. "Pencils have erasers to take away mistakes."

"Do most pencils have erasers?" Dad asked.

"Sure."

"Why?"

"Because everybody makes mistakes," Adam said.

"Everybody?" Dad asked. "You mean moms and dads and teachers and principals and ministers and friends and neighbors and famous football players and TV stars and presidents?"

"I guess so."

"Well, you guessed right," said Dad. "But what about you? Do *you* ever make any mistakes?"

"Yeah, me too, I guess," Adam grinned. "Once in a while—you know, *extremely* rarely."

"Right," said Dad. "You know some people can never admit that? But you can, and I'm proud of you."

Positive thought: Pencils have erasers because everybody, including me, makes mistakes sometimes. This doesn't upset me. I can learn from my mistakes.

Cured by a Bath

Each day after school, Butch's little dog greets him at the bus stop. But today as Snowball ran toward him, she looked different. She was a rusty red color instead of snowy white.

"I can't believe it!" Butch said to his friend. "What could have happened to Snowball?"

His friend, who had lived in Georgia much longer than Butch, knew exactly what had made the dog darker.

"She's red because of what she's been wallowing in," he said. "That red Georgia clay will do it every time. Nothing that a good bath won't clean up," he said.

People who have been "wallowing in" negative thoughts can take a mental bath to brighten themselves up. Thoughts like "I'm not good enough" or "I can't do anything right" can be washed away, just like the red Georgia clay.

First they imagine they are sudsing up their mind to wash out negative thoughts. Then they rinse them away. To finish, they add some positive thoughts—just like a cream rinse after a shampoo.

They brighten up from their thoughts just as Snowball brightened up after her bath.

Positive thought: I wash negative thoughts away and replace them with positive ones.

Cured by a Bath

The Big Decision

Laura had been taking dance lessons for seven years. This year she qualified for the special performing group. Many good opportunities were available to her as a member of the group, but rehearsals and performances took up a lot of time. She had two weeks to decide whether to join it.

Laura wanted to make the best decision. To help her think clearly about the situation, she labeled two columns at the top of a sheet of paper. The heading on the left column read "Yes." The other one said "No." Under each column she listed reasons for and against joining the special group.

While she was doing this exercise, Laura reminded herself that she could choose wisely.

"I just need to consider both sides of the situation," she said to herself. "Then I can think clearly."

After getting a good look at both sides of the issue, she made her decision.

Positive thought: I make good decisions.

Easy Answers

One look at eleven-year-old Keisha's face, and Dad knew she was upset.

"Middle school is so much to learn," she said. "Do you have any idea how hard it is to remember where you sit in seven different classes? And my books weigh so much my shoulders ache, but there's not enough time to go to my locker between classes." Keisha started to cry.

"Is there anything at all I can do to make you feel better?" Dad asked.

Keisha didn't even seem to notice Dad's question. She continued with her litany of problems. "Look at the size of my notebook," she said. "It's so big and confusing—just like school. If I just had little folders for each subject instead of this big thing to carry."

"Would they help that much?" Dad asked. Keisha nodded.

"Well, let's go. *That* we can take care of," Dad said.

They went to the drugstore and bought different-colored folders to match her different textbooks. The big notebook was donated to her little sister, who used it for play. Keisha was in a great mood for the rest of the day. In fact, two days later she said, "Those folders really made a difference, Dad."

Positive thought: Sometimes there are simple solutions to problems that seem really big.

The Judge

Mary Jo is a new girl at school. She has long brown hair and is really cute, but she acts like a snob.

When Debbie first met her, Mary Jo would hardly speak. Debbie thought she was stuck-up. "I'll bet she thinks she's cute," Debbie thought to herself.

As luck would have it, Debbie was assigned to be Mary Jo's reading partner.

During the next few weeks, Debbie began to know Mary Jo better. She learned that the beautiful brown hair was a wig. Mary Jo had lost her hair when she had chemotherapy treatment last summer. Mary Jo had been a very sick girl and was still in the process of getting better.

Her quiet way was not because Mary Jo was a snob. It was because she didn't feel well.

Debbie became Mary Jo's good friend. She felt bad for a while because of her mistake, but she learned a good lesson from it. She learned that judging people is not a good idea because it's hard to know what is really going on with them.

Positive thought: I agree not to judge people.

Bus Trouble

Madeline has a big problem every time she rides the school bus. The line to get off moves slowly and stops when she is right beside an older boy. Every day, Ricky pushes or pinches Madeline. She gets embarrassed, and the roughness hurts.

Madeline couldn't bear the thought of facing Ricky every school day all year long. It would be just awful!

She talked this problem over with her mother. "Maybe Ricky is being mean," she said, "because he's having trouble at home or in school."

"That may be," said Mom, "and understanding can help you. But you don't have to stand for his abuse. What can you do to protect yourself?"

"I already talked to the bus driver," said Madeline. "But she doesn't see what's going on. Now I'm trying to figure out a way to avoid Ricky."

The next day, Madeline thought of a solution. She stayed in her seat a little longer so some other children would get in line first. Now when the line slowed, she was standing beside someone else. The bus driver was watching and saw Ricky pinch a younger boy. After that, Ricky had to sit where the bus driver could see him.

Positive thought: I find the answer to my problems by focusing on the solution instead of the problem.

Too Much Homework

Zach was drowning in a sea of homework. He had a science project and a math quiz. Both were due tomorrow.

He was starting to panic about finishing everything.

"God," he said. "I know you are everywhere, including in me. I know I can do all this work because you are in me helping me."

After saying his prayer, Zach waited for the panic to fade. "I'll just do one step at a time," he said to himself. "That's what I'll do instead of worrying about all I have to do."

He began to feel calm and was able to do his work.

Positive thought: I can think in ways that calm me and help me with my life.

Letting Go of a Bad Day

Mom peeked in on Kris about an hour after bedtime. She had the covers pulled up around her, but her eyes were wide open.

When Mom leaned over to kiss her good night, Kris blurted out, "Mom, I can't sleep 'cause I'm just so mad."

Mom invited Kris into her bed to talk. And did she talk! What a school day she'd had. A bully punched her; another child dumped her crayons out "just to be mean."

When Kris had talked and cried it all out, she suddenly brightened. "You know what, Mom? When that bully wouldn't leave me alone, a girl I've always wanted to know better came and talked to me. She was nice too."

"Really?" Mom asked.

"Umhum. She's a neat person, Mom. Can I invite her over sometime?" After they agreed to do that soon, Kris curled up and fell asleep.

Positive thought: I help get rid of the bad things in my day by talking them out. Then I think about the good things. There's always *something* good in a day—even in a "bad day."

Jumpin' It Out

Alex felt a lot of anger when his parents separated two months ago. Since then, he has been in fights at school and has gotten in trouble with his teachers.

In a talk with the school counselor, he learned some ways to let his anger go without hurting himself or others.

Alex learned that physical exercise was a good way to release anger. He decided to jump on his trampoline every day to see if it would help him. He made up this rhyme to say while jumping:

Jump up and down
Jump all about
It's a good way
To let anger out.

In about a week, Alex noticed he was feeling better and getting along better with his teachers and classmates. He was jumping the anger out.

Positive thought: I can let go of angry feelings without hurting myself or others.

Alone Time

Mom encouraged both Janice and her little sister Justine to keep busy and take a lot of classes. "I always wanted to dance," said Mom, "but we couldn't afford anything like that."

So Janice and Justine belonged to the Brownies and the children's choir. And almost every day after school they took different kinds of lessons—ballet and tap dancing, piano and swimming.

One day when the girls' dance teacher was on vacation, Janice said, "Mom, it's so nice to have some time for myself. I just lay on my back this afternoon and imagined I was riding on a cloud, looking down at our street. It felt like a vacation."

"Hmm," said Mom. "Maybe you need to cut back on the activities. Would you like that?"

"What a relief!" said Janice. "To tell the truth, Mom, I don't like dancing much, but I thought I had to keep it up for you."

Justine looked amazed. "I've been wishing I could just come home and read sometimes or play in the leaves or go for a walk. I thought you liked the lessons, Janice, so I took them too!"

Mom laughed. "I've been spending every spare minute driving you girls to your lessons. I guess we've all been so busy trying to please one another that we forgot we all need some quiet time."

Positive thought: I balance my life by taking time out to be alone.

I Know What Works for Me!

Sean likes to play football, but his brother Eric prefers sitting on the dock, fishing and thinking. Holly surrounds herself with crowds of friends; the more the merrier, she says. But her neighbor Arlene feels happiest with one close friend who knows all about her.

Human beings are alike in so many ways that people speak of the "Human Family," but even the closest relatives also differ from one another. What works perfectly for one may not work at all for somebody else.

If something makes us happy and doesn't hurt anybody else, it's working for us.

Positive thought: I like being me and doing what makes me happy.

Dad's Turn to Learn

Susan came home from school with "bad day" written all over her face—in magic markers! She was convinced that her two best friends didn't like her anymore. They were spending all their time with a new girl. Susan was really hurt, angry, and lonely.

At the dinner table, Dad listened to all this. He told Susan how sorry he was. Then he just let Susan bounce everything off him. (Sometimes when you "bounce" a bad day off someone, it kind of "dribbles" away. Today, however, wasn't one of those days.)

Susan was still upset. She wanted to call one of her friends and scream and cry about how hurt she was.

Dad said, "Let it be. Don't do something you'll regret."

After Susan calmed down, Dad and Mom went for a walk. When they came back, Susan was whistling and full of pep.

"Dad, I called Kelly and Nan," she blurted out. "I told them how hurt I was, and they said they still like me a whole lot. They had no idea I was feeling left out. I feel just great, Dad. . . . But I didn't do what you told me to. I hope you're not mad."

Dad looked at Susan—but he was really looking within himself.

"Something in you knew what you had to do and how to do it," he said. "I got in the way by giving advice. I'm glad you can listen to your inner voice."

Positive thought: I follow my inner voice.

Staying Alone

Glen and Joe were both eight years old. Since they were neighbors and friends, their parents thought it would be a good idea if they began staying together for short periods of time without adult supervision.

One afternoon they stayed together for an hour while their parents were at a meeting. When they came home, the boys seemed fine. Later that evening, however, Joe told his father that he and Glen had actually been scared for a while.

"We heard a little noise in the attic right after you left," Joe said. "It was like someone knocked over some boxes or something. Then we were really quiet and listened and listened. We started to guess what made the noise and started imagining things."

"You seemed to be all right when we came home," Dad said to Joe. "What happened?"

"We finally decided to stop scaring ourselves, and we started to play. Pretty soon you were home. I'd like to try staying on our own again, Dad," Joe said happily.

Positive thought: I will not scare myself with my thoughts.

Project Breakdown

Jonathan felt that old overwhelming feeling creeping up on him again as Mr. Mackey assigned the social studies project on Hawaiian volcanoes.

His thoughts drifted. "How am I going to get this big project completed in just four weeks?" he thought. "I've started taking karate lessons and I have other subjects too."

Mr. Mackey continued to talk about the assignment and recommended that the students do a little bit of work each day on it.

Jonathan decided to give it a try. First he made a list of all the work he needed to do to finish the project. The list took a whole page. Then he broke this list up into smaller jobs like "Check out a book from the library" and "Make a volcano poster." He tried to arrange them in order of what needed to be done first. He decided to allow fifteen to thirty minutes each day to work on tasks for the project.

After a few days, Jonathan was in better spirits. He knew if he did a little work on the project every day he could handle it. Sure enough, he finished up in three weeks without a struggle.

Positive thought: I get big things done by breaking them down into small tasks.

"Paws" for Creativity

"'Paws' for Creativity" is the theme the children chose for Jeremy's creative writing class. His school mascot is a raccoon. That's where they got the "paws" from. Posters with raccoon prints line the walls to encourage kids to write creatively.

The phrase could also have another meaning. It could mean "pause" for creativity. To pause means to rest. People who are looking for new, creative ideas often take a break from routine thinking. This opens up their minds to fresh thoughts. A relaxed, rested mind is a creative mind.

One of the topics Jeremy's class wrote about was the many ways eggshells could be used. Jeremy thought of over forty ways to use them! He could crush and dry them, and then put them under a glass, like a mosaic. He also thought they could be used as sand in potting soil, if they were ground very fine. On and on the ideas came to him. He paused for creativity and the good ideas flowed.

Positive thought: Every day I can pause from my regular thinking and open up to creative ideas.

"Correct" Feelings

Ralph was talking with his father about feeling angry that the teacher had punished the whole class for a couple of kids' rowdiness. "To top it off," said Ralph, "Mr. Arnold told the class that we had no right to be angry!"

"I can see how it would bother you to hear somebody judge your feelings, as if he could decide whether you had a right to them."

"Yes! How can a feeling be correct or not correct?" Ralph asked. "A feeling is just what you feel. It's not right or wrong."

"I agree with you, Ralph," his dad said. "I'm going to try to accept my feelings too instead of judging them."

Positive thought: All my feelings are okay. They're my own, to be felt, not judged.

Focusing on Something Good

"I hate my face," Abby said to her friend as she looked in the mirror. "These freckles look so gross. I feel like one big freckle." She gave herself another look. "Hugh was calling me 'freckles' on the playground."

She stormed out of the school rest room, tossing her long brown hair over her shoulders. Her friend followed.

"Abby," she said, "you only have a few freckles. You're smart, and you have nice clothes. But *all* you talk about is how bad your face looks. I wish you'd think of something good about yourself for a change," she said as she walked into class.

Positive thought: Today I focus on something good about myself.

Slowing Down

Maggie was sick and tired of hurrying. She hurried to get dressed and out the door in the morning to school. After school she hurried to go to her piano lesson and then to do her homework.

But what bothered her most were her friends. All of them seemed to be in such a hurry to grow up!

"All the other girls wanted to do was talk about boys and makeup," she told her mother after a slumber party. "Marcie told them that I play dolls with my sister and that she saw me sitting on Dad's lap watching TV. They all laughed and called me a baby. We're only in the third grade! I *like* being a kid!"

Mom fluffed Maggie's curls with her hands. "It's healthy for you to enjoy being a child," she said. "You'll grow up when it's your own time."

Reassured, Maggie went outdoors with her little sister Allison. They raked the autumn leaves into the shape of a house with three rooms and played there until supper time. And when she went to bed that night, her doll was in her arms.

Positive thought: Today I give myself the gift of not having to hurry—for anything!

Laugh Lines

Anne adored Nancy, who was one of those kids that could send the class into gales of laughter whenever she opened her mouth. Sometimes she didn't even *say* anything. She just rolled her eyes, or gave a certain look, and everybody would be in stitches.

Anne was shy. She couldn't imagine telling a joke in front of the class if her life depended on it. Even so, the two girls became close friends. One day, Anne told Nancy how much she loved her sense of humor. "I wish I could be more like you. You make everybody else so happy," she said.

Nancy glowed, but she also looked surprised. "But one of the reasons I like *you* so much," she said, "is because you laugh so much. I love *your* sense of humor!"

A sense of humor is more than just being funny and telling jokes. It takes people with a sense of humor to laugh at the jokes too! Nancy has a gift: the gift of making others laugh. But Anne has a gift too: the gift of laughter.

Positive thought: I have a good sense of humor. I love to laugh.

Total Embarrassment

It was Judy's first day in her new school. She was really nervous. Moving to a new town after the school year had begun meant that she would be a stranger when everybody else had settled in with friends and routines. She wanted to do everything right today so she could blend in with the other kids.

Already, though, the day had started off wrong because she arrived at school late. Since she was late anyway, she decided to go to the rest room to fix her hair before going to class.

As Judy looked in the mirror to brush her hair, something strange caught her eye on the wall behind her. It was a toilet—on the wall. "Oh no!" she said. "I've done it now. I'm in the boy's rest room!"

Judy couldn't get out quickly enough. It didn't matter that no one had seen her. She was humiliated anyway—the kind of embarrassment that you just want to die from.

Judy went on to class and suffered all day. She couldn't quite get her mind off the rest room incident.

A few weeks later, Judy shared this story with her new friends. They squealed with laughter. Judy found she could laugh now too.

"Imagine that happening on your first day of school," she gasped between laughs. "I'm glad I can laugh about it now."

Positive thought: Laughter can help me get over my most embarrassing moments.

An Angry Day

Today Clay had an argument with his dad before he went to school. Riding the bus, he got into a fight with one of the kids over a seat. Then he got mad at the teacher about a math problem that she had marked wrong but he thought he had figured correctly. Walking home from school, he was kicking stones and still feeling mad.

Clay's anger was like a magnet. After his quarrel with his dad, he left for school full of angry feelings. These feelings pulled angry situations to him all day. The more he focused on the anger, the more anger came into his life. Anger is a powerful feeling, and it controlled Clay's entire day.

Positive thought: I let go of my angry feelings quickly so I don't spend the whole day being angry.

Fact or Fiction

Jeffrey was auditioning for the lead role in the school play. He was a good actor and was doing well on his tryout. Or so Jeffrey thought, until he saw his drama teacher frowning and fidgeting in her seat. She looked as if she couldn't wait for him to finish.

Jeffrey knew he had blown it now. On the way home, he made up a story in his head. "I know she didn't like my audition," the story began. "I'm sure I won't get the part."

When the phone call came, Jeffrey didn't even want to answer it. He just knew it wouldn't be good news. So when his teacher said, "Congratulations, Jeffrey. You won the lead part," Jeffrey was surprised, to say the least.

"But Ms. Johnson," Jeffrey blurted out, "I didn't think you would give me the part. During the audition, you seemed to be upset and rushing me."

At first, Ms. Johnson was puzzled. Then she said, "Oh, Jeffrey, I'm so sorry. A bug crawled across my foot right in the middle of your reading. I was upset because I wanted to go to the office and insist, once and for all, that they do something about our bug problem. It had nothing to do with you, dear," she said.

Positive thought: I look at the stories that I tell myself to see if they are fact or fiction.

A Simple Statement

Sometimes a simple statement like "I need to talk to you" can cause a pain in our body.

Gary's stomach began to ache when his teacher said those words to him at school one day. His first thought was "What have I done wrong?" He was worried and scared.

As it turned out, the teacher only wanted Gary to take home a note asking his mother to help with a class party. He hadn't done anything wrong at all, but still he had worried.

When Gary gave his mother the note, he told her about his stomachache.

"I know why that happens," she told him. "You probably don't remember, but whenever your father said that to you, he would yell at you or give you a spanking. He had a bad temper that he would not control. That's why he doesn't live with us anymore.

"Your body remembers all this, and that's why your tummy hurts when someone says that to you," Mother continued.

"Now that you are aware of it, you can tell your stomach to relax when you notice it happening. Just knowing what's going on will help you get over it," she said.

Positive thought: I can solve problems from the past so that they aren't problems in the present.

141

The Sponge

Human minds are like sponges, but instead of absorbing water, they soak up thoughts and the things that others say. Unlike the sponge, however, people can choose what they let their minds absorb.

When someone says something unkind about Andrew, he knows that he doesn't have to take it in. He tells his mind good things about himself instead.

And every night before he goes to sleep, he imagines he is squeezing out all the painful thoughts from his mind—just as he might squeeze dirty water from a sponge. Then he rinses his mind with good, helpful thoughts.

"I am okay," he tells himself. "I am a nice person and I feel good about myself."

Positive thought: I am in charge of what stays in my mind. I soak up helpful thoughts and squeeze out painful ones.

The Introduction

A popular children's writer was visiting Luke's school. Luke was chosen to introduce her at the assembly program because she was his favorite author.

He planned his introduction carefully. He went over and over it in his mind until he knew it well. He was feeling okay about it until the day before the author's visit.

When he told his brother how nervous he was, Will suggested that Luke say the introduction aloud a couple of times.

"Then you'll be comfortable saying it," his brother said.

Luke said Will's advice sounded silly. Will laughed and said, "Even the president of the United States practices with his aides before a press conference."

"I guess if it's good enough for the president, I can do it too," Luke said after he heard that.

Luke said his introduction in front of the mirror several times, and soon he felt comfortable saying it.

"It really helped me to tell you how I felt. Thanks for not making fun of me," Luke told his brother.

Positive thought: When I am nervous about something, I look for ways to help myself feel better.

Helping Your Doctor Make You Well

Jane went to the doctor this morning because she has a fever and a sore throat. The doctor gave her a prescription for medicine, which she will take three times a day.

"There are some other things that you can do to help yourself heal," said Dr. Foster. "While you're resting, close your eyes and imagine yourself playing and running happily with plenty of energy. Imagine that you're feeling good and having fun.

"You can also tell yourself healing things," Dr. Foster continued. "Say 'My whole body knows how to make me healthy. I can fight off this sore throat.' These thoughts will help you recover."

Jane has the power to help her medicine work.

Positive thought: Today I think about health and see happy pictures that help me to be well.

Relax the Hurt Away

Every time she went to the doctor's office for a shot, Glenda was so afraid that she almost became hysterical. She had to get more shots than most kids—two for allergies every Thursday.

One day Sue, the nurse, told Glenda something that helped a lot. She taught her how to relax by taking some nice, deep breaths. Then she told her to think about being at the beach: "Imagine the sound of the waves and the birds and the smell of the water."

"I don't know how I can think about the beach when I'm worried about a shot!" said Glenda.

"It does seem weird at first, but try it. Practice going to the beach in your head before you come back next week. You'll surprise yourself."

The following Thursday, Glenda was in a much better frame of mind. The shot didn't hurt as much. As she pretended she was on the beach, her muscles relaxed and the needle didn't feel half as bad as it used to.

"I can tell you've been spending a lot of time at the seashore," Sue said.

"I sure have," Glenda replied. "The shot didn't hurt half as much. I'm going to use my exercises the next time I have a sore throat or tummyache too."

Positive thought: Relaxation helps me feel better.

Soccer-Crazy

Brent was crazy about soccer. He lived it, slept it, and most of all, played it, every chance he could.

But Saturday, walking home from a game, he noticed that his best friend Charles had invited someone else over to play. Brent and Charles had always been inseparable—until soccer season started, come to think of it. It had been a couple of weeks since they had played together. Brent suddenly realized with a pang that Charles hadn't phoned in ages either.

Now Brent felt very lonely for his friend and the good times they used to have.

"I can't believe I didn't make time for my friend," Brent thought to himself. "I'm going to change that. I've got to find time for the things and people that I love the most."

He decided right then and there to ask his parents that night if Charles could come over the next day to play.

Positive thought: I make time in my life for the people who are important to me.

Life Balance

The drums rolled as the tightrope walker took his first step onto the wire. The only sound in the tent was the drum. When he reached the other side, the whole audience breathed a sigh of relief.

This part of the circus was Tony's favorite. "I just don't understand how a person can balance that well for that distance," he said to his dad.

"These people start practicing early in their childhood. And they practice every day," Dad said. "Balance is a funny thing because it's one of those things you take for granted until you lose it.

"Did you ever notice that if you give too much attention to one area in your life you feel fussy or irritable or even sick?" his dad asked. "That can be a sign that you're off balance."

"But how can a kid have balance when he has to be in school and do homework most of the time—that's what I'd like to know," Tony complained.

"The important thing is to make sure you get enough time for playing and relaxing," his dad said. "That's how a kid keeps balanced."

Positive thought: I keep my life balanced by taking time to play every day.

The Get-Over-It Box

Chandra has a shoe box decorated with construction paper. The box has a slit in the top, but it's not a valentine box. She calls it her "get-over-it" box.

Whenever Chandra has a negative thought she can't seem to get off her mind, she writes it down on a slip of paper. Then she puts the paper into her box. If that thought pops up again during the day, she simply says to it, "Now you're in the get-over-it box, and you have no power over me."

Using this box has helped Chandra get over ideas like "I always mess things up" and "I'm not good at math." Knowing a way to help herself in private allows her to make choices about her life.

Positive thought: The power for good—God—is the only power in my life. I use this power to help me get over thoughts that harm me.

The Sewing Doll

Sally thought long and hard about what to give Aunt Gail, her favorite aunt, for her birthday. Then she saw the perfect thing: a sewing doll. It was only two inches high and hung by a ribbon from sewing scissors.

Aunt Gail was always hemming or mending. "This will be a little surprise for her in the midst of her work," Laura thought. "It's a toy for grown-ups."

When Aunt Gail opened her gift, she oohed and aahed over the trinket. But then she said, "I'm going to put it on my little shelf of treasures instead of using it. It's just too pretty to use."

Two days later, however, Sally noticed that her aunt *was* using the doll.

Aunt Gail looked up from her stitchery. "You know, Sally, grown-ups have so many treasures they put away for company or safekeeping. I decided I loved this too much *not* to use it. I guess we never outgrow our need for toys," she said, winking at her niece.

Positive thought: I enjoy using my treasures.

Ending the Good Times

Star and Janet had been working together for two weeks on a special art project for school, a beautiful scene in a shoe box. It was such fun! First the brainstorming to decide what to make and how to do it. Then the endless phone calls back and forth to iron out details and share new ideas.

And then, of course, there were the hours spent working together cutting, pasting, sketching, and coloring.

Now the work was finally done. The two girls sat together, staring at the scene they had worked on so hard. Although they felt proud, they were both also a little sad.

"I'm already feeling lonely about not working with you anymore," Star said.

Janet nodded her head in agreement. Then her eyes brightened. "I know what," she said. "Let's just think of another project. But we'll make this one for us—not for school."

Star's face lit up, and the two girls bent over to discuss what their next creation would be.

Positive thought: When good times end, I can create more.

The Diary

"Dear Diary." Kathleen felt a little thrill as she wrote these words at the top of the first page of her new diary. Then she began to write furiously.

"I can't stand my new baby brother," she wrote. "I wish he lived somewhere else. All Daddy talks about is Scottie this and Scottie that. He doesn't even see me standing there. And Mom never has any time for me. Even when Scottie's not awake and screaming his head off, she's too tired to read to me. I wonder whether they'll remember my birthday next week."

Kathleen closed the book and locked it, feeling better already. As she put the key in her secret place, she thought, "Thank goodness for my diary. I don't always have to act nice when I write just for myself. I can write whatever I feel."

Positive thought: I can share my deepest secrets with my diary.

Nose Against the Window

Anne had her nose pressed against the window of the knit shop. The shop had suddenly appeared about two weeks ago in the store that used to sell dresses.

And it was a wonder to behold. The sunlit shelves were filled with yarn in more colors than in a giant crayon box. Hanging on the wall were beautiful, thick sweaters, perfect for this Minnesota chill. And in a cozy corner, several chairs were drawn together. Here women sat knitting and talking.

Anne took a deep breath. She didn't know what she was getting into, but she just had to go into this shop. It was as if someone had tied some of that yarn around her waist and just reeled her in like a fish. She *had* to learn to knit.

Anne felt that she had been chosen, drawn into a new creative adventure. She was overcome with the desire to create something. Other people might feel the same excitement when they draw a picture, build a go-cart, or master a new dance. The thing they end up with isn't the most important part. What really matters is creating, feeling that they are part of something much bigger than themselves. And they are.

Positive thought: I am a creative person. I inherited this from God.

Nose Against the Window

Mom's Miracles

M om had been really upset lately. She felt that she was always giving, and others were always taking. She didn't like the feeling that nobody even seemed grateful for what she was doing.

So she prayed. Just being clear about what was bothering her and turning it over to God always helped her. Then she decided that every time she caught herself getting angry, she would think a positive thought instead.

"My friends appreciate me and the things I do for them," she chose to think. "I love to be thanked, and I'm ready for it!"

Sometimes it seems we have to wait for what we want, but today was not one of those times. When Mom arrived at the synagogue for a volunteer job, she found that another woman had come early and finished all the work. Mom had once taken care of this woman's child when she was in the hospital, and she had chosen this day, of all days, to say thank you in her own special way.

When Mom returned home, she got a package in the mail from a friend she had picked up when he locked his keys in his car.

But the biggest surprise was yet to come. A man that Mom had done fund-raising for called out of the blue. He told her his company was giving Mom and the family a trip to Ireland.

That day, Mom learned not just to give but to receive.

Positive thought: I enjoy being thanked.

More Miracles for Mom

When Mother told the children about her day, they agreed that it had been filled with miracles. But she wanted them to realize that the biggest miracle of all wasn't the present from her friend, or the volunteer's gift of time, or even the free vacation.

"The biggest miracle was the change in my thoughts," said Mom. "I started attracting thanks because I started to expect that good things could happen to me."

Actually, people probably did appreciate Mom all along. But when she had assumed that everyone took her for granted, then she noticed only those who ignored her. Her "attitude of gratitude" made things change, because *she* changed.

"Before my miracle day," Mom told the children, "I was sort of like the little girl who didn't know her friends had planned a big surprise party for her. She thought no one liked her. But that wasn't true. They liked her so much, in fact, that they were at her house, hiding behind the furniture, waiting for the moment when she would walk into the room and they would all yell, 'Surprise, surprise!' But the little girl never heard them, because she never walked into the room.

"Today," Mom said, "I walked into the surprise party."

Positive thought: I believe that life is good for me and good to me. I expect that and accept that.

The World of Books

Cindy would never forget the day she fell in love with reading. Her parents had always read to her. When she was in bed at night cuddled up under the covers, the sound of Dad's voice reading a story quieted her and lulled her to sleep. And trips to the library were a family tradition—the book bag filled with colorful books; her own library card; and chatting with Mr. Simon, the librarian, who had—let's face it—*the* best job in the world.

But when she was ten, Cindy read a book, and suddenly, she *was* the book. This book happened to be *The Borrowers,* the story of a family of little people who live behind the baseboards in people's homes.

Cindy could not stop thinking about these elfin characters. She saw herself with tiny feet slipping into tiny leather lace-up boots. She imagined her whole world as it would appear to her if she were just two inches tall. Oh, she wished she could shrink to miniature size so she could be in the Borrowers' world.

It seemed she could not read fast enough. And yet, she felt she should slow down, so the book would never end.

Cindy would never forget that day: the day the magic of reading put her under its spell.

Positive thought: I have not just my own life to experience, but the life of every character in every book I choose to read.

I Can Accept

Lee's scout leader, Mr. Peters, noticed that Lee looked sad and invited him to talk about what was bothering him.

"I just wish I had friends and was popular like Ken," said Lee.

Mr. Peters said, "Sometimes I feel like you do. What I've learned to do is add one word to my thoughts: the word *accept*."

"I don't get it," said Lee.

"Life will often give you what you want and need, Lee, as long as it won't hurt anybody. But sometimes we stop good things from happening to us. We're sort of like people who love to give gifts but aren't very good at receiving them. Just try letting God know that you are willing to *accept* good things."

"How?" asked Lee, with a little more interest.

"You want friends?" Mr. Peters asked. "Every time you find yourself saying 'I want friends' or 'I don't have any friends,' instead say 'I accept friends into my life now' or 'I am ready for friends.' If you feel something is missing from your life, try opening yourself to new possibilities."

Positive thought: I am ready to accept whatever good I want in my life.

The Positive-Thinking Habit

"That positive-thought stuff just doesn't work," Don said to his good friend Melissa. "I tried it this week and it worked okay on Monday and Tuesday, but by Wednesday I was back to my old habit."

"What habit?" Melissa asked.

"Oh, being late for school," he groaned. "It seems that I've been a few minutes late my whole life! Every year the teacher talks to my parents about it. It's really embarrassing. I'm ten now, and I should be able to get to school on time."

"What were you doing to try to change?" Melissa asked.

"I just started thinking that I am always on time, especially for school. I was just so convinced I would get to school on time. And I did, for two days. But then I was late again," he complained.

"Don," Melissa said, "Don't be upset. If you've done something for five years, it might take a little longer than one afternoon to change the habit, don't you think?"

Don thought a moment and then said, "You're right. Positive thinking isn't magic. But if I practice it enough I believe I can get to school on time."

Positive thought: I follow up my positive thoughts with positive actions.

The Put-Down Person

Justin's mother asked him why he never invited Dennis over to play anymore. "You used to be such good friends. Did you have a fight or something?" his mother asked.

"It isn't like that, Mom," Justin told her. "Dennis has become a real put-down person. He makes fun of people a lot and is mean to them. You should hear how he talks to other kids. It's like he thinks he's better or something. I can't stand that!

"I don't play with Dennis anymore because I don't want to be around people who put me down. I'm choosing friends who build me up from now on," he said.

Positive thought: I choose friends who build me up.

The Balloon Express

One morning, Erica woke up with dark circles under her eyes. "Why, Erica, you look like you're about to cry," Mrs. Blumberg said. After looking at her daughter for a minute, she asked, "Is something bothering you, Erica? Didn't you sleep well last night?"

The words spilled out. "Last week Suzie made fun of my favorite doll, the one that Grandma gave me," she said. "She called me a baby and said I was too old for it. I really wanted to cry, but I wasn't about to let her see me. My feelings are still hurt," she told her mom.

Erica's mom told her about the time when her brother joined the Navy and went away. She had needed to cry, but she just couldn't. She held on to painful feelings and ended up getting kind of sick over it. She suggested that Erica do what she had done to get rid of those feelings.

Erica imagined loading all her hurt and angry feelings into the basket of a big, colorful, hot-air balloon. Then she gave the balloon a big push. Up, up, and away it went—far out of sight.

"Do that again whenever the hurt comes back," Mom said, "and I know you'll feel better."

"I already do feel better, Mom," Erica said. "When the balloon went up, my anger went with it."

Positive thought: Letting go of hurt feelings always makes me feel better.

159

A Hairy Morning

Jackie was struggling with her hair this morning. "I hate my hair," she said, throwing the brush on the floor.

Jackie's hair was very thin and straight as a board. Her new haircut had really looked good at the hairdresser's, but today it was a mess!

"Can I help?" Mrs. Maxwell asked her daughter.

But Jackie was at the age when one minute she wanted her mom's help, and the next minute she didn't.

"How could you help?" Jackie asked. "This will take a miracle."

"You'd better be getting in touch with the miracle department soon because we have to leave for school in fifteen minutes," her mom said.

Jackie laughed, and her mom rummaged through the hall closet until she found the curling iron. They fussed and sprayed, and together they came up with a cute style.

"Looks like I've found the miracle department right here in my own bathroom," Jackie said. "Thanks, Mom."

Positive thought: It's okay to let others help me. I appreciate it when they do.

I'm Satisfied

The cabin was very cold when the family arrived there in November. It had been sitting empty and boarded up for months and felt like a refrigerator.

But Dad had laid a fire in the fireplace before they left the last time, preparing for their next arrival. Soon a glorious fire was crackling and popping away. The children snuggled up in front of it. Letting the fire's warmth seep into their bones, they discovered the true meaning of "toasty warm."

At that moment, no one had any desire or want or need outside of this room, this fire. They were satisfied.

How nice that some things can be totally satisfying, even if only for a short while: a fire on a cold day, warm cookies and cold milk after school, a comfortable old armchair for reading, a new set of crayons, watching a cat preen and lick itself. That's satisfaction!

Positive thought: I can think of many pleasures that comfort and satisfy me.

Hot-Water Bottles and Sidewalks

Ellie had gone with her father to Scotland. Her grandpa was ill, and they wanted to see him. It was the first time in eleven-year-old Ellie's life that she had been out of the country—or even California, for that matter.

Her mom couldn't wait to find out what had made the biggest impression on Ellie. Was it the highlands, with their wild, rose-colored heather and woolly sheep? The strange and charming accents? Riding trains and double decker buses?

Now that she was back home, Ellie mentioned all these things and more. She loved Scotland. But the sights that had made the biggest impression were everyday things. Hot-water bottles and sidewalks! Her grandparents' home, like most in that country, had no central heat. Nor did it have electric blankets. So a hot-water bottle placed between freezing cold sheets at night was a special treat, especially for a girl far from home.

And the sidewalks enabled her to walk to the store for shopping. Here in her suburb, cars were the only link to the malls.

Hot-water bottles meant being warm and safe. Sidewalks meant freedom to explore. Sometimes the simplest things in life give us the most pleasure.

Positive thought: I get a lot of pleasure from simple things in life.

Thank You

"What's something good that you like people to say to you?" Mr. Watts asked his Sunday school class. He thought they would like to be told that they were good-looking or smart or nice.

To his surprise, Margie said immediately, "I like to be told 'Thank you.'" Another child agreed and the whole class nodded.

"Sometimes adults are so busy with other things that they forget to thank their kids," Mr. Watts said. "It may be a good idea to let your parents know how good it makes you feel to be thanked.

"And I'll tell you a secret," he added. "The more you say 'Thank you,' the more you will find people thanking you."

Positive thought: I like to give and receive thanks.

Coming Home

Four children are on their way home after a busy day at school. One is blond, limber, six-year-old Katie. She loves school, but as she rounds the bend to her home, she picks up speed. She is excited about the gymnastic pad in the basement. She can't wait to start doing somersaults and straddle rolls.

On the next block, nine-year-old Colleen opens her back door, gets safely inside, and lets out a deep breath. She loves the familiar "house smell" that greets her as soon as she opens the door. Some boys teased her on the way home. It scared her, and she is glad to feel safe and sound.

Across town, eleven-year-old Ron waves good-bye to the bus driver and runs across the dirt yard he and his neighbors in the housing development share. His mom works, so Ron lets himself in with his key. "It just feels so good to be home," he thinks to himself as he flops down on the sofa.

But seven-year-old Rachel enters *her* door in tears. She's had a fight with her best friend. "Mom," she cries. "Wait till you hear about the day I had."

Home means many wonderful things to children. It's a place to play, a place to feel safe, a place to relax, a place to find comfort.

Positive thought: I am thankful for my home.

Mind Grooming

In addition to using the mirror to style her hair or check her appearance, Rhonda has another use for it. Every time she walks past a mirror, she takes a moment to stop and look herself in the eye and say something good about herself. She calls this "mind grooming."

One day Rhonda was chosen to make a presentation to the teachers at her school. A few minutes before her talk, she went to the rest room to do mind grooming for confidence. She looked at herself in the mirror and began talking silently. "I am sure I will give a good talk. This is going to be fun."

Just then, Mrs. Barton stopped in to wash her hands. Rhonda felt a little embarrassed, but the teacher said, "Oh, hi, Rhonda. I'm introducing you at the meeting, so I stopped in here to get ready. Before a big moment, I like to look myself in the eye and say how capable I am. It builds me up."

They went down the hall together, and Rhonda sat next to Mrs. Barton at the meeting, feeling that they were comrades.

Positive thought: I can build confidence in myself.

The Day Grandpa Died

Frank lay in the big four-poster bed all day long. Ever since the call came that Grandpa died, Frank didn't want to see anyone. He would cry for a while; then he got angry at all sorts of people. At the doctor for not saving his grandfather. At all the people visiting and talking so loudly. Even at Grandpa. They had planned a fishing trip together. Now the only trip would be to the funeral home.

Later that day, Frank's dad came in and sat down on the bed. Frank talked about all of his feelings and his dad listened hard.

"These mixed feelings happen when a person grieves," Dad said. Frank was relieved to know these feelings were normal.

"I remember when my mother died. I was furious at everybody. I was even mad at God. That *really* felt awful," Dad said.

"One reason we feel so bad when people die is that we're afraid we didn't express our love to them enough, especially if we had a fuss with them before they died," Dad said. "After my mom died, I wrote her letters telling her my feelings. All of them—love and anger. Then I imagined that I was my mom and wrote a letter back to myself. Strange as it sounds, that helped me a lot."

The thought of writing to Grandpa appealed to Frank. He could have a "Diary to Grandpa." He would write in it for a long time.

Positive thought: People I love can help me get through the pain of grief.

The Stars Get Up

The ice stadium was pitch-dark as Carol and the rest of the crowd waited for the Olympic stars to enter the spotlight. Out came the woman who had won the gold medal. Her energy on the ice kept all eyes locked on her. Then the men's champion skated out. What enthusiasm he showed as he danced on his skates. What graceful moves!

But then the whole crowd gasped as he lost his balance and skidded across the ice. Carol was horrified with embarrassment. "Falling down in front of a few people is embarrassing enough," she thought, "but to fall down in front of thousands would make me want to crawl in a hole."

But then, almost as fast as she could blink an eye, the skater was back up on his feet. He glided, he twirled. His skate blades flashed and the spangles on his blue costume glittered. At the end of his beautiful performance, his skates threw up a spray of ice crystals, and he raised his arms in triumph.

The crowd roared its admiration.

Positive thought: When I make a mistake, I quickly pick myself up. Being a winner doesn't mean I don't make mistakes. It just means I always get back up again.

Making Pot Holders

The kids could hardly sit still. Thanksgiving had passed and the holidays were coming. Looking through an old toy chest, trying to find something to do, Mick found two old toys. They were small plastic looms used to make pot holders.

"Look," he said to Eileen, "let's do this."

And they did—by the hour. Each went through a mound of cloth loops, picking green and white ones for a teacher, solid yellow loops for a neighbor, several colors for a plaid for Grandma.

In one day each child made several lovely pot holders. It was as if they had woven all the frenzied anticipation of gift giving into those little squares. And indeed, it was true. Their gifts were as cheery and bright as the holidays. The fingers that had made them had woven their excitement into each one.

That night the children stacked up their pot holders. They couldn't wait to see the grown-ups' faces when they received these presents. The frenzy was gone. In its place was the spirit of giving.

Positive thought: My energy is creative. I can create things of joy for others.

Making Pot Holders

The Emergency

At the top of the hill, the car engine stopped. Mr. Bishop tried and tried to start it up again. No luck.

"Must be out of gas," he grumbled. "I'll put the emergency brake on and walk to a filling station. You kids stay in the car and don't get out for any reason."

Six-year-old Sandy thought about all the things he had seen on the TV show *Emergency* and wondered what was going to happen.

After Dad had been gone awhile, Sandy's big sister Marie noticed Sandy was crying. "What's wrong?" she asked.

"I'm afraid of the emergency," Sandy replied.

"What emergency, Sandy?" his sister asked.

"The one Daddy put on the emergency brake for. I don't know what it is and I'm scared," he said.

Marie couldn't help laughing a little. Then she quickly explained to Sandy that the brake *avoided* an emergency by preventing the car from rolling downhill.

Getting the right information helped Sandy feel safer. He and Marie sang some songs, and before long, Dad returned with a can of gas.

Positive thought: Finding out as much information as possible helps me be less afraid.

Sharing Love

"Everyone likes to feel loved and accepted," Rob's teacher told the class. "But sometimes people are in such a hurry that they don't take time to express love. After school today, think of four things that you can do to show your love."

That evening, Rob cut out a heart from a sheet of notebook paper and put it in Dad's lunch bag. He thanked Mom for cooking meat loaf and mashed potatoes for supper. He complimented his friend Alyssa for her catch in a softball game. And he tied his little brother's shoes.

The next day at school, Rob thought of one more thing to do. "Thanks for helping me think of ways to show love," he wrote on a note to his teacher. The things I did made me feel happy, and other people showed their love back to me with smiles and hugs."

Positive thought: Today I think of ways to share my love.

Sick of Being Sick

Jeannie had been home sick for one week. She had been getting plenty of rest and liquids and had taken the medicine the doctor had prescribed. But instead of feeling better, she seemed to be getting worse.

Then one morning when Jeannie asked to watch television, Mom said, "No. Instead, I want you to get out a pencil and paper. Write down all of the things you're going to do for fun once you're well."

Jeannie grumbled, but she found that she actually enjoyed thinking about fun. "I will go to school to see my friends," she wrote. "I will play hopscotch and ride my bike."

"Jeannie, every time you get an ache or pain today," Mom said, "I want you to read over your list. Let yourself *feel* how good it is to be well again." And Jeannie did.

The other thing Jeannie did was repeat these sentences aloud several times during the day: "I'm starting to feel better. I have more energy every day."

Sometimes sickness can become a habit. Jeannie realized that she missed the good times she had when she was well. Soon she was back at school, feeling like the old Jeannie.

Positive thought: My mind can help me feel better. When I'm sick, I like to think about the fun I'll have when I recover.

People of All Ages

April loves her grandmother dearly. She loves her grandmother's friends too. They're very kind and lots of fun.

Once April begged to go on a senior citizens' trip with her grandmother. April said she'd put on a silver wig and high-heeled shoes and go around saying "I'm an old lady" to prove to people that she belonged on the trip.

Finally, Grandmother asked April exactly why she liked being around her friends so much.

"You always take it easy and enjoy whatever you're doing," April replied. "That's what I like about you!"

Positive thought: I enjoy being around people of all ages.

The Art of Living

Most children love art. Some of the nicest things about it are the ways it differs from other school subjects. There are no simple, right-or-wrong answers in art. A teacher can ask the students to draw a picture of a man with a hat, and each picture will be unique. One is not right and all the others wrong. All are right. They are art.

Life is like art—at least more like art than math or spelling. Each of us wants to express life, but we do it in our own individual ways. One person wears brightly colored clothes, another faded blue jeans. One likes to skateboard, another to fish. One prefers classical music, the other jazz. And none of us is wrong. We're just practicing the art of living.

Positive thought: I am an artist at life. I express myself in many creative ways.

I Create Special Things

Fran made a beautiful clay pot in her Girl Scout troop meeting. She put a blue-gray glaze on it. She was so proud of her new creation . . . until she took it home. Then her older sister Sara said it was an ugly piece of junk.

Fran began to look at it a little closer. Now she noticed that it had little mistakes and flaws here and there. Her face fell. Maybe her sister was right.

Then Fran smiled and took a long, deep breath. "No," she thought, "this pot is beautiful. It's special to me because I put myself into making it. Whether Sara thinks it's beautiful doesn't change its value to me."

Later Sara apologized to Fran. It turned out that she had been upset about something else when she made those comments about Fran's pot.

Positive thought: I am pleased with what I create.

Feeling Good

Jenny and her family were sitting in the living room listening to the *Phantom of the Opera*.

Jenny loved this music and how it made her feel—even when she felt tears stinging her eyes at the sad parts.

She felt the same way when she read a line in a book that described a feeling she'd had. Or when a friend started to say something and Jenny could finish the sentence for her and they would laugh together.

"I just love life right now," thought Jenny. "I absolutely love it."

Positive thought: I enjoy so many things about living.

Mom's Crabby

Mom was *really* crabby. She knew it too. She'd say she was sorry and give Tara a hug. Then ten minutes later, she'd snap at her again.

Tara tried to talk to her mom about it. Usually Mom liked to talk through conflicts, but not today. She just shook her head.

Tara felt confused. She knew that worrying wasn't good for anybody. But what do you do when someone you love is upset?

Finally she decided that she could help her mother by thinking positively about her. Here are some of the thoughts that Tara kept repeating to herself that day instead of worrying about her mom: "Mom has a problem, but she'll be okay," Tara thought. "No problem is too big to be solved. Mom's problem will be solved. She is strong enough to handle this. No matter how bad things seem sometimes, they work out all right."

It felt so good to help her mother—and herself—in this way.

Positive thought: I respect others' feelings and moods. I can't always help them, but I can think good things about them.

Money, Money, Money

C hip was eight years old, and like other eight-year-olds, he was very interested in money: allowances, the cost of things, the way checks and banks work, money matters of every kind.

So Chip's ears perked up when he heard his parents talking about money. It was near Christmas, and his folks were discussing plans to save during the next year.

"I think we spend too much time talking about money," said Dad.

"What do you mean?" asked Mom.

"Talking about what we want or need is like thinking about what we *don't* have, instead of what we *do* have," he said. "Let's just have a year of being thankful for what we do have and just *enjoy* it, not think about how we can get more."

Positive thought: Thinking about what I *don't* have makes me worry. Thinking about what I *do* have makes me thankful.

The Christmas Tree

Ten-year-old Amy was hanging ornaments on the Christmas tree. She always liked decorating the tree, but this year it was more fun than ever because she recognized different ornaments that people had given her over the years.

Here was a hand-knit teddy bear. It had been a gift from a baby-sitter six years ago. And here was a little brass angel, given to her by a neighbor where they used to live. And here was one Grandma had given her. And this one was from her new neighbor.

Suddenly Amy realized that the tree meant a lot more than a place to put presents under. This tree held memories of past Christmases, past friendships, her life. All these little things that friends had given her made the tree into a Christmas tree.

Positive thought: What my friends have given me continues to be a part of me. And I continue to be a part of their lives through what I have given them, even when we don't see each other anymore.

The Christmas Solo

Rita was supposed to sing a solo in the church Christmas program. She had expected to be nervous, but she hadn't expected to be scared stiff.

When it came time to sing, the worst possible thing happened. She opened her mouth to sing, and nothing came out. *Nothing.* After a few seconds, the teacher realized what was wrong. She led the whole group into song to cover Rita's mistake.

Rita couldn't wait for the program to be over. She always loved all the Christmas cookies and treats after the programs, but not tonight. All she wanted was O-U-T. She searched the audience for her mom and dad. But when she found them, she didn't dare look them in the eye. She was afraid she'd start crying.

Later, at home, she *did* cry. Dad held her and just kept saying, "There, there. It will pass, honey. Just get it out." She cried until her sides hurt and she felt that there wasn't a drop of water left to be squeezed into a tear.

Then Dad said, "Rita, I want you to know that we are proud of you. You didn't do anything wrong or bad tonight. You just lost your voice and got embarrassed. But Mom and I are proud of you all the time, not only when you succeed. We're proud of you for trying."

Positive thought: Sometimes a bad thing happens. When it does, it's okay to cry and seek comfort. Bad times pass.

What Goes Around Comes Around

Megan gave her grandmother a special bookmark for Christmas. It was brass, with a butterfly that perched at the top of the page when the book was shut. The butterfly's wings were enameled with royal blue, red, and yellow.

It was a perfect gift for her grandmother because she read so much.

When Grandmother opened the gift, she smiled.

"I gave a similar one to a friend of mine," she exclaimed. "And I really hated to part with it. The old saying 'What you give away always comes back to you' really came true in this case, didn't it, dear?"

When people give of themselves, their time, their talents, their allowance, they may not always see the "brass butterfly" in return. But it is there. What we send out always comes back to us many times over.

Positive thought: What I give makes others happy. Then it returns to me, multiplied many times.

The Boredom Cure

"I'm so bored," Manuel said as he flipped the television channel from station to station. "Reruns!" he huffed. "Only reruns."

Like Manuel, all boys and girls are bored from time to time. Manuel knows a cure for boredom that helps him and his friends.

First he talks to himself. He says, "My mind is full of fun ideas." He repeats this to himself several times.

Then Manuel gets a piece of notebook paper and writes down whatever ideas come to his mind. They can even be outlandish or silly ideas that he knows he couldn't possibly do right now—like sailing on an ocean cruise. Writing down these ideas opens up his mind to many creative possibilities. In some way, they help him come up with his own personal boredom cure.

Eventually, he thinks of things he can do right now. Maybe a walk in the woods. Or making a costume for his favorite action figure. Or reading a book and pretending he is one of the characters.

Positive thought: My mind is filled with creative ideas. I use them and I am not bored.

Christmas Jealousy

Hank and Spencer received bicycles for Christmas and spent the next week riding them. Both boys were having a good time showing their parents the things they could do. But something got in the way of the good time Hank was having. It was that old feeling of jealousy. He had always been a little jealous of his younger brother. He felt his parents gave Spencer more attention. And now it was happening again—right here at Christmas.

For a long time, Hank tried to hide his jealousy. He hoped it would just go away. But feelings aren't usually like that. They usually don't just disappear.

Finally Hank decided to let himself feel really jealous for a while. He got into it "big time." When he thought he was about to burst, he told his parents and his brother what he was feeling. He almost felt guilty doing this.

What Hank did was take a chance. It was risky telling his parents and his brother because he didn't know how they would react. He didn't want them to think badly of him.

The amazing thing was that after Hank expressed his feelings, he felt that he was in control of them again.

Positive thought: Trying to hide my feelings only makes them grow. I express my feelings, and that helps me to be in charge of them.

Giving Yourself a Present

Theresa likes presents so much that sometimes she gives one to herself as a special way to say "I love you, Teri," or "I'm proud of what you've done."

When she has saved her allowance, she can buy herself a candy bar or a colored pad of paper. But she can also give herself something she *can't* buy.

One quiet, private present she sometimes gives herself is a pat on her own back when she's done something that was hard for her. For example, when she finally raised her hand to answer a teacher's question at school, she was very pleased with herself. She told herself so: "I'm proud of myself," she said. "No one but me knows how hard that was for me."

Another present she gives herself is "Thanks." She figures that if she thanks others, she can do the same for herself, her first best friend.

Positive thought: I'm proud of me. I'm going to remember to tell myself that.

Other titles that will interest you . . .

My Body Is My House
A Coloring Book About Alcohol, Drugs, and Health
by Jeanne Engelmann, illustrated by Patrice Barton
    As children color these drawings and read the simple self-care messages, they'll learn how to care for their bodies as they would a house, by keeping it strong and by keeping out things that could hurt. This 8-1/2" x 11" coloring book helps children ages 4 - 9 discover that the things that keep their bodies strong are fun to do, too. 15 pp.
Order No. 5100

Wonder What I Feel Today?
A Coloring Book about Feelings
by Jeanne Engelmann, illustrated by Patrice Barton
    Learning about feelings is fun when you have pictures of other kids to color and rhymes to read! This 8-1/2" x 11" coloring book helps children associate facial expressions and common experiences with words for feelings. While coloring and reading, kids learn to express their feelings. For home or classroom. Ages 4-9. 16 pp.
Order No. 5177

For price and order information, or a free catalog, please call our Telephone Representatives.

HAZELDEN EDUCATIONAL MATERIALS

1-800-328-9000
(Toll Free. U.S., Canada, & the Virgin Islands)

1-612-257-4010
(Outside the U.S. & Canada)

1-612-257-2195
(FAX)

Hazelden Educational Services International
Cork, Ireland
Int'l Code + 353-21-961-269